Dorrie's Book

By Marilyn Sachs

Dorrie's Book

BY MARILYN SACHS

Drawings by Anne Sachs

DOUBLEDAY & COMPANY, INC.   Garden City, New York

Library of Congress Cataloging in Publication Data

Sachs, Marilyn.
  Dorrie's book.

  SUMMARY: An only child relates the trials and tribulations she experiences
when her mother has triplets.
  [1. Family life—Fiction] I. Sachs, Anne. II. Title.
PZ7.S1187Do   [Fic]
ISBN 0-385-03350-8 Trade
      0-385-03213-7 Prebound
Library of Congress Catalog Card Number 74-33688

For my friend and editor, Barbara Greenman

BEFORE

I have nothing against King Arthur.

As a matter of fact, I read the stories a long time ago, when I was eight or nine, and not this easy, watered-down version either with all the Thees and Thous turned into Yous, and nothing about the guilty love between Launcelot and Guinevere.

They were nice, pleasant stories too, and I hope Mrs. Lyons isn't taking any of this personally. I am learning a lot from Mrs. Lyons, and if I ever grow up to be a teacher, I will know many things not to do. For instance, when Mrs. Lyons started handing out copies of King Arthur to the class, and some of the kids moaned and said, "Why do we have to read this, why?" and she said, "Because in this school, *everybody* in the seventh grade *has* to read King Arthur," she should have stopped right there. Most kids understand that there is no point in arguing once a teacher says, "Because *everybody has to!*"

But Mrs. Lyons didn't stop. She is a very popular teacher, and she wants her students to enjoy themselves. That is one of her problems. So she went on talking, explaining how she believed the stories were very exciting, and that they showed how man (and woman) hadn't really changed that much down through the ages. How people had always struggled against fear and injustice and other problems, just the way they still do—even though nobody lives in castles any more or wears armor.

9

I guess I'm responsible for starting it all up again because I was thinking of my own problems, and they had absolutely nothing to do with giants or green knights without heads. So I said, "But, Mrs. Lyons, King Arthur isn't relevant."

Then Sharon Low got into it, and said, "Yeah, King Arthur isn't relevant. Drugs *are* relevant," Sharon said, "so how come we can't read something interesting and relevant about drugs like *Go Ask Alice* or *Dinky Hocker Shoots Smack?*"

Again, Mrs. Lyons could have stopped the whole thing by just repeating that all seventh graders *had* to read King Arthur. But she believes that students are people and should be listened to. So she listened to Jeff Parsons who said that King Arthur wasn't relevant since nobody fought with swords and bows and arrows any more. Nowadays you drop napalm or bombs, and he thought the class should read *M*A*S*H* or some other good war story.

Arthur Prendergast mentioned that his older sister had read King Arthur, and said that it was the most boring book she ever read. After that, everybody seemed to have something to say, and Mrs. Lyons was listening to all of them.

It wasn't long before Jeff Parsons said that even he could write a more interesting book than King Arthur. Mrs. Lyons said that she didn't think he could, considering how much trouble he had with one-page book reports. But Jeff said he could and would rather write a book than read King Arthur.

Again, Mrs. Lyons could have handled the whole thing by telling Jeff to be quiet and sit down. But she didn't. Instead, she tried to point out to him how much longer it would take to write a book than to read one. But Jeff kept insisting he could do it, and after a while, he brought his copy of King Arthur up to Mrs. Lyons' desk, and she said, OK, if he was silly enough to prefer writing a book to reading one, she would accept it.

Sharon Low, Steve Bosco, Alex Fink and Karen Miller brought up their copies too.

"All right then," Mrs. Lyons told them, "but we're going to

lay some ground rules. When I say a book, I don't mean two or three pages with large writing on one side."

Marina Driscoll brought her copy up.

"And don't think I'll accept the usual stuff I get from you about 'My cat's name is Fluffy. She is black and white. She is very friendly.'"

Susan Gin and Frank Harris brought up their copies too.

"Remember," Mrs. Lyons said, "that if you don't read King Arthur, you won't be able to take the two tests I plan to give and the three word quizzes. Which means that your entire end-term mark will depend on your book. It will have to be a real book too—a long one with chapters, and a plot, and developed characters."

Three more kids came up to her desk.

"You won't have a chance to make changes. I'm not going to allow any mistakes in spelling, grammar or punctuation. Your book will have to be free of any errors, just as if it was a printed book."

When I brought my book up, Mrs. Lyons looked at me, kind of puzzled. She said, "I know there are some people in this class, Dorrie, who will do anything to get out of reading. But why you?"

I could have stood there and explained that I had already read King Arthur so I wasn't really trying to get out of reading it. I could have also explained why King Arthur was just not relevant to my problems, but I decided that maybe my book would do it all much better. So I didn't say anything. I just laid King Arthur on her desk, and after school, I hurried home, and began.

Dorrie's Book

Chapter One

My mother had three miscarriages before I was born. Then she had me.

"I don't know why you keep asking me about them," she used to say. "There are lots of other, happier things we can talk about."

"But I want to know what they looked like. Weren't you even curious?"

"No, I wasn't curious. I was just miserable."

"What did it feel like—I mean having a miscarriage? Did it hurt?"

"Yes, it hurt—and I hope it never happens to you or to anyone else I know, or to anybody for that matter."

"But, Mom, how did they happen? Did you do something wrong?"

"No, they just happened."

That's the way our conversations about her miscarriages always started—with me asking lots of questions, and her trying not to really answer. But after a while, I'd get her going, and she'd start.

The first two miscarriages happened almost as soon as she became pregnant, but the third one came in her third month. It was a boy. They could tell even though he was only a couple of inches long, a teeny, tiny boy. My little brother. His name would have been Randolph.

When Mom got pregnant with me, the doctor made her quit her job and stay in bed most of the time. They hired a woman to come in and do the cleaning, and stay with her

15

when Dad wasn't home. Dad did all the shopping and cooking and made things like gazpacho and jambalaya. But Mom said she couldn't eat anything at first. All she did was cry and throw up Dad's gazpacho and jambalaya. But that lasted only for three months. After three months, she stopped crying, began to eat, and started worrying. She was afraid I might not be normal. Between eating, worrying and reading books about all the different ways I might not be normal, she kept busy for the next six months.

Then came the part I liked best.

"But what time was it?"

"I've already told you—in the middle of the night."

"But what time exactly was it?"

"Oh, about two."

"Two what?"

"You know. It was two-fifteen."

"Go on! Go on!"

"Well, I woke up and my water had broken, and the bed was soaking wet. So I began to get up, and . . ."

"No, not yet. You woke Daddy first."

"That's right. So I said, 'Charlie, Charlie, my water broke,' and he said, 'Don't worry about it, I'll be all right.'"

No matter how many times Mom told the story she always had to stop and laugh. "He really used to dream that he was having the baby. And I'd hear him groaning."

"And then what happened?"

"Well, I had my suitcase all packed and waiting."

"What was in it?"

"A robe, slippers, nightgown, some cologne, powder for me and some baby things."

"What baby things?"

"You know what baby things."

"Please, Mom, don't leave anything out. You always leave something out."

"All right—let me see—a pair of diapers, a little undershirt, a baby kimono . . ."

Mom's suitcase → Mom's robe

mom's nightgown

cologne

Powder.

Baby Things (or Me Things)

= my diapers   my undershirt

and

MY KIMONO

"What color?"

"White. We didn't know whether it was going to be a boy or a girl—and a beautiful crocheted sweater and hat with yellow ribbons that Aunt Kate made for you."

"She didn't make it for me. She didn't know it would be me."

"Well, it was you," Mom said, really warming up to the subject now, "and when they held you up to me, and said, 'Congratulations, it's a girl,' I thought I'd . . ."

"Mom—stop! You're leaving everything out."

She always left something out. I knew the story better than she did. Sometimes it felt like I was remembering it all. Like I was there myself. Naturally, I was there, but I mean like I knew everything that was happening. The drive to the hospital at three in the morning with the city streets dark and empty, the bright hospital with nurses and doctors running up and down the corridors, Mom lying in the labor room with Dad pacing up and down outside. Up and down for six hours.

"How is she, Doctor? Is everything all right, Nurse? How is she, Nurse? Is everything all right, Doctor?"

There I am, pacing up and down outside with Dad, lying in bed inside with Mom, hurrying into the delivery room with the doctor, adjusting my mask with the nurse, and finally screaming my head off with me.

"It was worth it," Mom always said. "All the waiting and worrying—it was all worth it."

I thought so too, because they might have ended up with something like Adam Frost or Karen Cook. Not that I'm really all that special although the way they used to talk about me you'd think I was the most beautiful, brilliant, sweet-tempered child that was ever born with the possible exception of one other. And maybe they wouldn't even exclude Him. I guess I'm smart all right. I've been in a special program in school ever since I was seven. It's called MGM, and doesn't have anything to do with the movies. It stands for Mentally Gifted Minors, which means that I'm smarter than 98 per cent of all kids my age. It's not always easy to explain this to some of the 98 per centers. Jody Jamison once put her face right up close to mine, and said it was a lot of bull about me being smarter than 98 per cent of all the other kids my age. She said they just picked those kids who weren't good at anything else and who most people couldn't stand, and tried to make them feel good by saying something nice about them.

Which is not true, but I didn't want to argue with Jody Jamison because she was so big and mean. I'm smart all right, but I don't think I'll ever be pretty. Mom is pretty—slim and graceful, with large blue eyes and soft, shiny red hair. I wish my hair was red instead of brown, and that I wasn't so short and chunky.

"Bunny," Dad always called me, "my own special Easter Bunny," because I was born on Easter Sunday, and also (I don't like this part), because I'm fat and round like a bunny.

"There's only one thing," Mom always said, "one thing that I'm sad about, because no child should grow up alone. I had your aunt Kate, and Daddy had his three brothers . . ."

"But you always said how Aunt Kate used to tease you, and Daddy said Uncle Jim and Uncle Tony never talked to each other, and Uncle Edward once hit Daddy so hard with his skate that it ripped open his leg, and he needed twenty-seven stitches."

"Yes, but when you have brothers or sisters there's always somebody to depend on, and later, when you grow up, why you're a family with nieces and nephews to enjoy."

"But Aunt Kate is in Providence, and we hardly ever get to see her or her kids, and Uncle Tony and Uncle Edward are in Silver Springs, and Uncle Jim . . ."

"Well," Mom admitted, "it would be nice if they were closer, although I really can't stand Tony's wife, and Kate does have her moments, but the important thing is whether you're near or far, you're still a family. I wish you could have the experience of a brother or a sister, but it doesn't look as if that will ever happen."

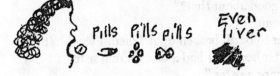

Nothing had happened to Mom since I was born. Not even a miscarriage. She went to the doctors, took pills, and vitamins. She and Dad even went on a special protein diet where they ate liver for breakfast. Nothing helped.

When I was seven, Aunt Kate and her three girls came to
visit during the summer. "There's always prayer," Aunt Kate
said to Mom. "It's no good for a child to be alone. No good
for her, and—just in case—you understand what I'm talking
about, Maureen, no good for you. All your eggs in one
basket—that's asking for trouble."

I asked Aunt Kate what she meant by saying, "All your eggs
in one basket—that's asking for trouble." But she just said I
should go play with Alison. Alison is her youngest daughter
and exactly my age. Alison didn't understand what all your
eggs in one basket meant, and neither did Margaret who was
nine. But Elizabeth, who was twelve, understood.

"It means that if you die, your mother will be all broken up
because she doesn't have any other children."

"But Aunt Kate didn't say anything about dying. Just
about a bunch of eggs in one basket."

"Look, stupid," Elizabeth explained slowly, "what happens
if you drop a bunch of eggs in one basket?"

"They all break."

"Congratulations. OK, now if you put some of the eggs in
one basket, and some in another, and maybe some in a third
. . ."

"I understand," I said. "It's like if you died, Elizabeth, your
mother wouldn't care so much because she'd still have
Margaret and Alison."

"That's right."

"Well, what's so good about that?"

"What do you mean?"

"I would want her to be all broken up if I died. I wouldn't
want her to feel better because I had a brother or a sister. I
don't want a brother or a sister."

"Oh, stop it! You're just a self-centered little brat."

"I don't want a brother or a sister," I shouted. "I don't
want to die, and have a brother or a sister sleeping in my bed,
and making my mom feel good." I must have been screaming
because Mom came running in, and so did Aunt Kate. When

they heard the whole story, Aunt Kate said, "You see!" to
Mom, and Mom started going to church after that and
praying.

   But it didn't help.

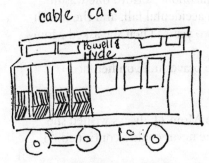

cable car

Powell &
Hyde

Ghirardelli
Square
Hot Fudge
Sundae
YuMMMy

Poor Mom wanted another baby so badly, and everybody
seemed to rub it in. Wherever we went, there was always sure
to be somebody who didn't believe in only children. Even
strangers. One day, on the cable car, Mom was taking me
down to Ghirardelli Square for hot fudge sundaes. We were
talking and laughing, and an old lady next to Mom smiled
and said, "They're so sweet at that age, aren't they? How old
is she?"

   "Eight," Mom said.

   "Lovely child," said the woman, and then sighed. "Enjoy it
while you can. Mine are all grown up now and out of the nest.
Ah, how I miss them!"

Mom nodded, and everybody was quiet for a moment. I was just going to ask Mom if we could walk over to the Municipal Pier after we ate our sundaes, and see if anybody was catching fish when the woman started telling Mom about her children—all four of them. One of them was a student in Arizona, and seemed to be hanging around with a fast crowd, another one was married to an alcoholic, a third one was in the hospital recovering from an accidental fall, and the fourth one she hadn't heard from in two years. Then she asked Mom how many children she had.

"Just Dorrie," Mom said, the brave smile on her face.

"Just the one?"

"Yes."

There was a silence, and then Mom (I always wished she would sit out the silence, but she never could) continued. "I wanted more, but . . ."

"What a shame!" said the lady.

"Yes," agreed Mom.

"Have you tried . . ."

"Everything."

"Tsk, tsk," said the lady, shaking her head. "Have you ever considered adopting a baby?"

"How come," I continued the question after we got off, "that you never did adopt another baby? I mean, if you really wanted one."

"Because I always hoped we'd have another one of our own. And now that I know we won't, I guess Dad and I just feel it's too late."

"You know," I said, "just in case you'd like to know what I think—I never wanted a brother or a sister."

"Well," Mom sighed, "if you'd had one you'd feel differently."

"Most of my friends hate their brothers and sisters. Lisa Schwartz says she wishes her brother was dead."

"People say things like that but they don't really mean it."

"And one day, she tried to make him run across the street when the garbage truck was coming."

Mom laughed. She didn't believe me.

"It's the truth, Mom. And it's also the truth that I never really wanted a brother or a sister."

We were walking up the steps into the square, and I stopped because I realized that what I had just said wasn't exactly so.

"Well, maybe I did want a brother."

Mom nodded, the brave smile on her face again. "I'm sure you do."

"No, not do, did. I wanted Randolph."

"Who?"

"Randolph. My little brother who died. He's the only one I really wanted. Only he wouldn't be my little brother, would he, Mom? I mean he'd be seventeen months older than me, so I'd be his kid sister."

Mom squeezed my hand. She never seemed to think about Randolph the way I did. Mom said that sometimes miscarriages happen because there's something wrong with the baby, and it's nature's way of keeping a person who's not normal from being born. Sometimes it's all for the best even though you can't help feeling sorry. But I never thought of Randolph as having something wrong with him, like Peter Basque whose tongue hangs out and whose mother has to take him across the street even though he's fourteen. I could even see Randolph as a tall, slim boy with light brown hair and large blue eyes, a lot like Dad. Very friendly, with a big smile on his face for me. Sometimes I even missed him, and once I cried because we'd never be together, and he would never know what it felt like having me for a sister.

Soon Mom and I were sitting at a table with huge hot fudge sundaes sprinkled with nuts in front of us. Soon we were busy working our way down through the whipped cream and the double scoops of vanilla ice cream and the thick, thick fudgy sauce, and I stopped feeling sorry for my brother, Randolph.

Chapter Two

Dad always made the salads, large, green, leafy ones with plenty of Bermuda onion rings. Sometimes, and this was my favorite, he made Caesar salad.

We all had to be sitting down at the table for the performance. Our round oak table in the kitchen would be set with the blue and white dishes, the blue mug of milk for me, and glasses of red or white wine for my parents. There were always flowers because Mom said she couldn't enjoy a meal without flowers. At least twice a week she stopped at Jack's Flower Shop for shasta daisies, daffodils, carnations, or small pink roses.

shasta daisies

daffodils

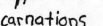
carnations

pink roses

In the winter, when darkness came earlier, we ate by

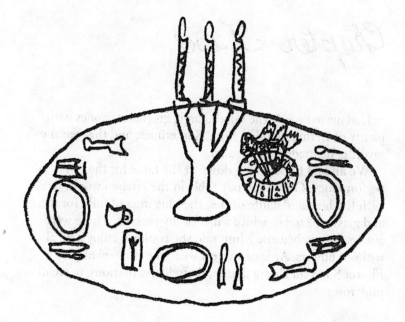

candlelight, and had the lights of the city outside our window unless the fog hid them from us. Best of all was when it stormed, the rain streaming down outside the window, and inside, the three of us sitting warm and snug together around our bright table.

There was music too. Most likely Bach or Vivaldi, or perhaps, if Dad had his way, Christopher Parkening playing Villa-Lobos on the classical guitar. It was the happiest time of the day for me, and I think it was for them too.

Dad's salad always came first. He generally stood when he was making it, a serious look on his face. Sometimes, Mom and I smiled quickly at each other, but we never let him see. If it was the Caesar, he had all the greens already tossed in the oblong rosewood bowl that had come from Africa. In front of him, like a surgeon's supplies, lay small bowls of anchovies, croutons, salad dressing, grated cheese, and one egg. First he put in the anchovies and tossed carefully. Then the croutons and the salad dressing. The egg was the main event. He cracked it against the side of the bowl, raised his arms, and broke it high above the salad so that we could watch its descent. More tossing, and then finally the seasonings and grated cheese.

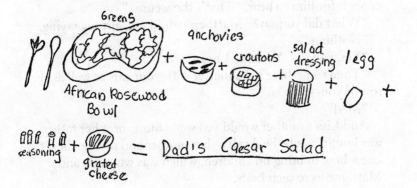

Dad could cook too, mostly interesting dishes with foreign names like Arroz con Pollo or Coquilles St. Jacques. Often, during school holidays or on weekends when he wasn't so rushed, he'd plan a whole surprise meal and chase both Mom and me out of the kitchen. Not that I could cook at all. Up until I was eleven, I didn't do anything in the kitchen or any place else in the house.

Dad is a principal, but he looks like a movie actor. He is the only principal I ever saw who looks like an actor. Most of them are skinny and nervous. But my father looks like a taller, older, and—believe it or not—better-looking version of Robert Redford. And I am not the only one who thinks so either. Most of my friends used to flip over the way he looks. Debbie Mason used to say that both of my parents look like they should be in the movies. Then she'd look at me and laugh in a mean way.

In those days, neither of my parents ever raised their voices. Not to me, and not to each other. It was something I never told anybody. It was too embarrassing. Maybe I'd spend the afternoon at Lisa Schwartz's house, and her mother would come in and shout at her every fifteen minutes or so because she dropped her things all over the place. Then Lisa would wait until her little brother, Matthew, came by, and she'd look at him, and say to me in a low voice that was loud enough for him to hear, "That's the weirdo."

"What did you say?" Matthew would ask, already crying.

"Nothing."

"Yes, you did. You did. I heard you."

"Then something's the matter with your ears as well as the rest of you—weirdo!"

"MA!"

And Lisa's mother would yell some more, or if her father was home, maybe he'd yell at her mother and say she didn't know how to bring up children, which was why Lisa and Matthew were such brats.

But at our house, nobody really argued. Only how could I say so to Lisa or Debbie or the other kids who had normal, unpleasant families.

Even the place we lived in was special. It was a large, two-bedroom apartment up in the Twin Peaks section of San Francisco. There were two balconies in the apartment. One of them was more like a deck, and it lay outside the sliding doors

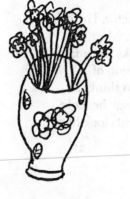
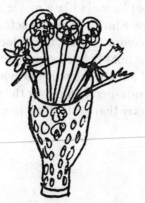

of the living room. There were colorful clusters of geranium, fuchsia, and periwinkle standing around in bright Mexican pots. Mom had picked up some old metal garden furniture and painted it all white. In the warm weather, we often ate breakfast or lunch there, and sometimes on weekends we would just stay home and spend the day reading and sunbathing on tatami mats. The view from that balcony was over the city and out to the Bay Bridge. You could see the tops of schools, houses, and hospitals. You could watch the traffic moving along Market Street and Van Ness. It was the same view we had from the kitchen.

The other balcony lay outside my bedroom. It was tiny, just large enough for me, and maybe a friend if we squished. But I could see out over Golden Gate Park to Golden Gate Bridge and the Marin hills behind it. In the summertime, I could watch the fog roll in from the sea. I loved to sit outside on my balcony when the weather was warm enough and read, or lean on the railing and know that all of it down there, the people, the cars and the trees, even the fog—all of it belonged to me.

View From my Bedroom

My room was small but just right for me. One wall was painted a deep blue, and the other walls were white. Against the blue wall was my bed with its shining brass posts, and my blue, green, and yellow patchwork quilt from the mountains of Kentucky. Mom and Dad bought it for me one Christmas when I was nine. At first, I was disappointed—a quilt wouldn't seem like much of a gift to most kids. But later, I came to understand not only how expensive it was but how it was full of wonderful stories. The lady who made the quilt, Mom said, was very old, nearly ninety, and famous for her beautiful designs. Each little scrap of material came from a wedding dress, a baby's shirt, a pair of curtains or a sun bonnet. Many of the pieces were old too, older even than the lady. All sorts of different people with all sorts of different stories had given a piece of their lives for my patchwork quilt.

Whenever I was sick and had to stay in bed, I could be absorbed for a long time with my quilt. All I had to do was shut my eyes, pass my hand up and down, and finally stop. Whatever patch my hand rested on was the one I told myself a story about.

There were bookshelves in my room filled with my books and my games. One special shelf was reserved for my collection of foreign dolls. There were twenty-three of them, and they gave Mom so much pleasure collecting for me that I never had the heart to tell her that I really stopped being interested in dolls by the time I was nine. My desk was a small, roll-top oak desk with carved drawers. Mom had picked it up in a secondhand store and refinished it. I loved it, even though the roll top usually got stuck, and I had to leave it open most of the time.

Our whole house was bright with colors—mostly blue, white, gold, and orange. There were two sofas in the living room, both white with orange and gold pillows, and a large blue Persian rug on the floor. All the wooden furniture in our place was old. Mom and Dad loved poking around secondhand stores and buying hideous painted, broken pieces of furniture that turned out to be beautiful antiques after my parents finished rubbing, polishing and repairing them.

Most people thought our place was beautiful. Then, I never thought about it. Now I know it was. All the great views from the windows, the bright colors, the old, special furniture, and the plants and flowers everywhere. Mom was a great housekeeper too. Of course, Mrs. Olsen came in twice a week to clean, but it never seemed to me that there was anything that needed cleaning on the days she did come. Mom was always so busy keeping things neat in between.

When I was seven, Mom went back to work as a nursery school teacher, but she was always home when I got back from school. She loved to bake, and the wonderful aromas of fresh bread or cookies or chocolate chip muffins always seemed to greet me as I ran up the stairs after school.

mom bakes

cookies

breads

muffins

etc. etc. ...

When I was very little, Mom and Dad left me with baby
sitters whenever they went out. But as I grew older, they
began taking me along with them. Sometimes it was
dinner—generally in one of the small, out-of-the-way foreign
restaurants. Sometimes it might be a movie, and then as I
grew older, a play. When I was eight, I started going to
concerts. At nine, I saw my first opera, and by ten, they took
me everywhere. I knew all the museums in the city and was
particularly fond of the netsuke collection of tiny ivory statues
in the Brundage.

"Precocious" was a word I heard a lot from Mom's friends.
I looked it up in the dictionary, and discovered that I was
either "Forward in development, esp. mental development" or
"bearing blossoms before leaves." Another word I sometimes
heard was "obnoxious." Which means "Annoying or
objectionable due to being a show-off or attracting undue
attention to oneself."

The first time I remember hearing it was at a dinner party
my parents gave when I was about seven. Although I did not
eat dinner with their guests as a rule, they always liked to have
me mingling while they all had drinks. This particular
evening I sat down near Mrs. Rommenberg, a teacher in my
father's school, and explained to her why Oaxaca was a more
interesting town than Guadalajara. She had just returned
from a week in Mexico, but since our family had spent a
whole month there during the summer, I felt I could point
out a few features she might have missed.

That was the first time I heard the word "obnoxious." Mrs.
Rommenberg said it to Mr. Henry who was sitting next to
her. She said it in a low voice, the same kind of voice Lisa
Schwartz used when she called her brother, Matthew, a
weirdo. So I suppose Mrs. Rommenberg wanted me to hear.

After that, I sometimes heard it from other people, but it
never bothered me. If I mentioned it to Mom or Dad, they'd
generally laugh.

"She's just too much for your friends to handle," Dad might say to Mom.

"What do you mean, *my* friends? Were you there when she told Fred Cummins that he was mistaken about Point Reyes being a state beach, and that it was really a national recreation area?"

"Too much, too much," Dad crooned. Maybe by this time he'd grabbed me, and sat me on his lap on the big, old Shaker rocker in front of the fireplace. "What a smart bunny it is!" Maybe it was after dinner, and there was a fire in the fireplace, and Mom was sitting on the sofa, knitting a sweater for me. Maybe it was one of those clear, sharp nights when the sky was as black and deep as the city lights were white and sparkling. Maybe we talked and laughed as the evening passed.

That's the way I like to remember us. Back in those wonderful, happy days. Back when I was still an only child.

Chapter Three

All the time we were in Hawaii that Christmas when I was ten, Mom didn't feel well. Usually at home she was the first one up in the morning. It always gave me a happy feeling to hear her quick footsteps in the hall, and the clatter of dishes in the kitchen while I still lay deep and warm under my blankets. It makes getting up in the morning a little bit easier if somebody else does it first.

But in Hawaii, Mom never felt like getting up in the morning, and she didn't want to eat breakfast. At home, Mom was always forcing oatmeal or bacon and eggs down our throats, and telling us how breakfast was the most important meal of the day. But in Hawaii she'd sit at the table, watching us eat with a sick look on her face.

"Maybe this is what they call jet lag, but it's never happened to me before."

She took naps in the afternoon, lying out on the beach, and usually by nine o'clock at night she was ready for bed.

"I think you're not getting enough iron," Dad suggested one morning. "Now that you're middle-aged, like the man says, maybe you've got iron poor blood. Time for Geritol, or maybe liver and oysters."

"I'm only thirty-eight," Mom said, looking green, "so I have another two years before I'm officially middle-aged, and—please—don't say liver and oys . . ."

Sometimes she barfed.

35

There was a movie once that Mom and I watched on TV. It was about a woman who thought she was pregnant and went to the doctor. But instead of being pregnant, it turned out she was dying of cancer. With my mother, it all happened in reverse. One night after we had returned from our trip I heard Mom crying. She and Dad were in the living room, and the sound of her sobbing woke me up. I opened the door to my room and, terrified, began moving slowly toward the living room. I stood there in the doorway, but at first they didn't see me. There was only the fire in the fireplace, and the room was dark. Mom lay crying on the sofa, and Dad was on his knees, bending over her.

"But now—Maureen, darling, stop crying—you really have to go to the doctor. You can't put it off any longer. Why didn't you tell me you were so worried?"

"No, no, no," all muffled from my mother.

"I had no idea that you were so worried. My darling girl, stop crying like that."

"I'm almost positive," Mom cried. "It's the same symptoms—no appetite, nausea, headaches, I'm losing weight, I look yellow and peaked. Poor Joe had the same symptoms."

Joe Porter was a friend of my parents who had died of cancer in the fall.

"How can you be so silly, Maureen?" Dad asked. "Let me call the doctor tomorrow. I'll even go with you. I know it's nothing to worry about."

"If you know it's nothing to worry about, how come you'll take time off from school to go with me? You haven't missed a day in years," my mother wept.

"Just an hour or so. I'm not worried at all," Dad said in that hearty voice he used at graduation programs. "I just know you're worried, and I also know you'll feel much better once the doctor says it's not that."

"Well," cried my mother, "if it's not that, what is it?"

But by that time, my father had seen me standing there,

and by that time I was crying as loud as my mother, and everybody had to get busy comforting everybody else, and saying how sure they were that it was nothing.

I hurried home from school the next day, and I was scared. Joe Porter had been a big, husky man who laughed a lot and never said I was obnoxious. He had died around Thanksgiving, and although I hadn't seen him, I knew from what my parents said, in low, scared voices, how he'd lost nearly one hundred pounds, and died a shrunken shadow of himself.

All the way home from school I felt the terror in my throat. A couple of blocks away I started crying and running at the same time. If my mother lost one hundred pounds what would be left? She wasn't much more than one hundred pounds as it was. Gasping and crying, I dragged myself up the stairs. There was no good baking smell. I burst into the house screaming, "Mommy, Mommy, Mommy!" I hadn't called her Mommy since I was little.

She came running from her bedroom, and grabbed me, kissed me and said, "What is it, darling? What happened? Are you all right?"

"It's not me," I shouted. "It's you. Are you all right?"

"Oh!"

My mother pulled back from me, and looked, smiling, into my face.

"It's not cancer?"

"No, no, sweetheart. No, no! Nothing like that. Something very different."

"Oh, Mom," I cried, "I was so worried. Oh, Mom!" I hugged her and she hugged me, but she wasn't finished. I looked up at her and smiled. Of course, I couldn't know what was about to happen to me.

Mom burst out laughing, sat down on the floor, and said, "Something very different. Very, very different, and very wonderful. The best thing in the world. Dorrie, darling, I'm—we're going to have a baby."

37

Right from the start I never thought it was "the best thing in the world." The real best thing in the world is being an only child and having two parents who think you're the greatest. The best time in my life was when I was an only child, and nobody can tell me it's because "you don't have any brothers or sisters, and you just don't know." I know.

I always knew. As soon as she said it, I knew. I was suddenly terrified, so frightened I couldn't even say anything.

Generally, Mom always knew how I was feeling. I wouldn't even have to say anything but she seemed to know what was happening inside me. When Lindy Cooper bit me that time I sat on her sandwich, even before I told her about it, Mom said, "What's wrong, darling?" She could always tell from my face.

But not this time. She was so busy, laughing and talking, it was as if she suddenly stopped seeing me. It was scary. And I didn't know how to tell her it was scary. The next few days all she seemed to do was giggle—on the phone when she called up all her friends, and her friends' friends, and just about anybody who'd listen.

"Crazy, isn't it?" (giggling). "You'd think a woman my age would know the classic symptoms of pregnancy" (more giggles), "but, honestly, I'd stopped even thinking about it for several years, and, of course, my periods were always irregular. But when Dr. Tolland told me there was no doubt, I said," (lots of giggles) " 'You've got to be joking,' and he said . . ."

Mom kept saying "we" were going to have a baby, but I was never fooled. It wasn't going to be my baby.

"Maybe, darling, you'll finally have a real brother named Randolph."

"But, Mom, I already have a real brother named Randolph. Only he died seventeen months before I was born."

"It would be wonderful if we had a boy, but then if it was a girl, you'd have a sister, just like Aunt Kate and me. What do you think of the name Deirdre?"

"I hate it."

"That's what I really wanted to call you, but then I reread all the Greek myths while I was pregnant with you, and Pandora just seemed right. She was the first and only girl in the world, and that's the way we felt about you when you were born."

Lots of times, she didn't seem to hear what people were saying to her. She was busy inside herself, with her own private thoughts, and they had nothing to do with me.

One night, right in the middle of dinner, when Dad was saying how the water kept backing up in the playground drain in his school every time it rained, Mom announced, "I'm so happy." She reached over and took Dad's hand, and then she reached over and took my hand, and smiled at both of us with a dreamy, inside look on her face.

"You've got your elbow in the butter, Mom."

"I'm so happy."

"So am I," Dad said, smiling back at her.

"Why is everybody so happy?" I asked. "Just because the drain in the playground keeps backing up, I don't see what's so great about that."

Mom laughed and squeezed my hand. "I'm happy because I've got you, Dorrie, and Daddy, and now we're going to have another baby, and our family will be complete."

"I always thought our family was complete."

Dad understood how I was feeling. Maybe he was feeling a little scared too, because later he talked to me about Mom. He said Mom was the kind of person who had lots of love inside her. Just because she was having another baby, Dad said, did not mean that she would love him or me any less. In fact, according to him, she would probably love us even more, which was not quite clear to me. He told me how much Mom had wanted another baby, and who could blame her since I made her so very happy. He said the new baby was going to be really lucky—not only in having such a wonderful, loving mother but also in having such a sweet, generous eleven-year-old sister who could take care of him or her, play with him or her, read to him or her, and, above all, love him or her. He kept talking about how mature I was and what a great help I was going to be. I knew he was trying to make me feel important, and I think he knew I knew he was trying to make me feel important. I was still scared but suddenly I wanted to be important. I guess I let myself be brainwashed.

The doctor thought Mom should quit her job immediately and stay home. He was afraid there might be the danger of another miscarriage. Here is where I really began to feel important. At first, Mom wasn't supposed to go up and down the stairs or do any housework at all. Mrs. Olsen came in three times a week now, but I began running all sorts of errands for Mom. I went to the grocery, the library, and the

Grocery snopping

Book Picking

Yarn Getting

knitting store. I bought beautiful pale green wool for her to make a baby sweater and cap. She taught me how to knit, and on warm days, the two of us sat outside on the large balcony knitting. Whenever Mom felt thirsty, I'd bring her some juice or a glass of milk. If the phone rang, I answered it.

At the library, I picked out all the books on babies I could find for her. At first, she was the only one who read them. Then Dad did, and finally me. There was one that showed what the baby looked like while it was growing inside its mother. It looked like a little caterpillar at the beginning, but by now—we figured our baby was about ten weeks—it already had a face and eyes, and funny, little stubby fingers with no nails.

Gradually, I found myself growing excited about the baby, although I was still scared. I began to care what it was going to be called. Mom held firmly to Randolph if it was a boy and Deirdre if it was a girl. Dad liked Randolph too for a boy and Rebecca for a girl. I liked Raymond for a boy and Elizabeth for a girl.

"When can we go shopping and buy baby things," I kept asking.

"After a while," Dad said. "And if Mom still can't leave the house, then you and I will go and pick everything out."

But Mom was able to leave the house by the end of her third month. The doctor decided that she was in such good condition that he thought it would be safe for her to try going up- and downstairs, and doing some light housework. If everything continued to go well, there was no reason why she could not resume all her normal activities.

"What I really want to do," Mom said, "is take a natural childbirth course and do all those exercises. I'd love to have this baby naturally. And Dr. Walker, even though he is such an old-fashioned doctor, really approves of natural childbirth."

When she was in her fourth month, Dr. Walker said my mother could resume all normal activities. She registered for the natural childbirth course and started wearing black leotards and sitting lotus fashion on the living-room rug. She and I did leg exercises together and practiced deep breathing, using our diaphragms. In natural childbirth, the father is generally present at the birth. My mother promised to ask her doctor if I could be present too. He said no.

Mom and I decided to make birth announcements. We made it look like a little coloring book. On the first page, I drew a picture of a man smiling. Over him, I wrote:

THIS IS
CHARLES O'BRIEN

Color His Shoes Brown
And His Tie Yellow

The next page showed a woman with a great big smile. It said:

THIS IS
MAUREEN O'BRIEN

Color Her   Hair Red

The third page showed a girl without such a big smile. She was drawn a little bit slimmer than she should have been. Over her, it said:

THIS IS
DORRIE O'BRIEN

Color Her Eyes Blue
And Her Shorts Green

The next page had no drawing, just words that said:
THEY WOULD LIKE YOU TO MEET
THE NEWEST MEMBER OF THEIR FAMILY
And then, when you turned that page, there was a picture
of a smiling baby with a blanket up to its chin. Next to the
picture I wrote:

THIS IS

OR

RANDOLPH   DEIRDRE

color ____ Blanket
____

We could have all the announcements printed up except for the three blanks on the last page. We'd have to fill that in later. If it turned out to be a boy (and if Mom got her way), we would write:

THIS IS <u>RANDOLPH.</u> COLOR <u>HIS</u> BLANKET <u>BLUE</u>
  If it was a girl:
THIS IS <u>DEIRDRE.</u> COLOR <u>HER</u> BLANKET <u>PINK</u>

Even though I was still scared, I began to get used to the idea. I'm sorry to admit that I had a strange preference for a brother even if he did steal his name from my poor, little dead brother, Randolph. I could see myself pushing him in a new, elegant, low carriage, and all the kids crowding around to look at him and me. I could see myself holding him in my arms and feeding him, playing with him, protecting him, rescuing him from an earthquake, and teaching him to read when he was only three. He would love me the best in the family, even more than Mom and Dad, and later, when he grew up and had problems, he'd come to me and I'd always know how to help him.

Chapter Four

In the beginning of her pregnancy, Mom told me that she wouldn't begin to "show" until about her fifth month. But in the middle of her third month, even though she still wore ordinary clothes, you could tell that she was having a baby.

We went shopping for maternity clothes. Mom bought pants with stretchy fronts for her belly to grow into. She

bought three tunic shirts and a long blue shimmering dress that looked like a tent. She bought floppy nightgowns and underwear that was a couple of sizes too large for her.

Baby Clothes (for Mom)

Even though I wasn't pregnant, Mom thought I needed something new too. So we bought me a pair of blue pants, a bright red turtleneck shirt, and a red and blue plaid jacket with big, shiny white buttons. Later, we had lunch in a Mexican restaurant, and Mom said she was going to have to watch her weight. In a way, Mom said, it was too bad that she had stopped being nauseous. Everything tasted so good now, but she was afraid she was gaining too much weight.

& Me

In her fourth month, she gained eight pounds, looked very pregnant, and was scolded by her doctor and put on a salt-free diet.

In her fifth month, Mom's belly stuck all the way out. My mother is ordinarily a small, very slim woman. The rest of her still looked small and slim, but her belly just didn't seem to match. It looked as if it belonged to somebody else, a much bigger woman, and that Mom was just looking after it until its owner came back to claim it.

"I don't know," said my mother. She wore her maternity clothes all the time now, and had bought a roomy jacket and two more pairs of pants in a larger size. "Last time, when I carried Dorrie, I hardly showed until the sixth month, and even in my eighth month when I wore a coat, you could hardly tell."

"Aren't you supposed to be bigger with each baby?" Dad asked.

"I guess so, but I'm really huge, and it's not even the end of the fifth. This is going to be some big baby."

We spent a lot of time thinking about where the baby would sleep. None of us wanted to give up our beautiful apartment. Eventually, Mom said, we'd have to find a place with another bedroom, but she thought for the first year or so, anyway, the little dressing room next to their bedroom could be converted into the baby's room.

"I never want to move from here," I told Mom. "Never! I love it here. I love my room and my balcony. There's no place I'd ever want to be but here."

Mom smiled. "It is a lovely place, Dorrie. But you don't have to worry. We won't move to any other place unless you love it just as much as this one."

"Promise?"

"Promise."

In spite of the salt-free diet, by the end of her fifth month, Mom had gained seven pounds. Dr. Walker was also suspicious.

Mom looked tired and worried. "He said that I'm much bigger than I should be. He wants me to come back in a couple of weeks. He says there seems to be another sound when he listens to the baby's heartbeat. It could mean that there's just the possibility of twins."

"Twins!" Dad was drinking a Bloody Mary and sitting on the couch. Mom was sitting next to him, and I was on the rug in front of him. Mom had told me the whole story when I got home from school, and I couldn't wait to see Dad's face when he heard. Mom made me promise not to go running up to him when he came home and blurt the whole thing out. She wanted him to have a chance to relax a little before she ruined his evening.

"Twins!" Dad put his drink down.

My friends and I sometimes play a game called "Statues."

50

You say, "Make a face of a person who's just swallowed a worm in an apple" or "Make a face of a boy who's just been spanked," and everybody has to make that kind of face. The one who makes the best one gets to be "It."

Anyway, if I'm ever asked to make a face of a man whose wife has just told him she might be having twins, I'd know how to do it. First you jerk your head forward as if somebody

just hit you on the back of your head. Then you twist your mouth down on one side, wrinkle your forehead, widen your nostrils, and turn red. Maybe I couldn't manage the turning red unless I held my breath, but I could do all the other things.

"Of course he's not absolutely sure, but he just might be hearing two heartbeats. You know he's old-fashioned about using equipment like X rays or even that new sonar thing, but he's sure in a couple of weeks he'll be able to hear . . ."

"Oh sure," Dad grumbled, "he's so hard of hearing, I'm surprised he can hear anything."

Mom began crying.

"Now, Maureen," Dad said, putting an arm around her, "if he upsets you like this, I think you should change doctors."

"He isn't upsetting me," Mom cried, "you are!"

A few weeks later, Dr. Walker said he could definitely hear two heartbeats, and congratulations, it *was* going to be twins.

My father was not happy.

"We'll have to move and right away," he said. "We can't stay here with two babies."

"Well, we're not moving now," Mom said. "We'll wait

until after the baby, I mean babies, are born. I just couldn't manage a move now."

My father was not happy at all.

The strange part of it was that I was fascinated by the idea of twins. I had seen that spooky movie *The Other*, all about

DREAMS
OF
MULTIPLE
BIRTHS

STUCK-TOGETHER
(SIAMESE)

BEWARE!!
THE OTHER

SWORD
OF
BLOOD

these identical twin boys. One of them dies, but because they had been so close, the living ones becomes sort of possessed by the spirit of his dead brother. There were lots of neat stories about identical twins.

"Do you think they'll be identical?" I asked Mom.

"I don't know. There are no twins on either side of the family so I couldn't say."

"That's what's so unusual," Dad said. "I just don't understand how this could have happened. There's no history of twins, and it's supposed to run in families. Do you think all those pills that nutty doctor gave you all those years could have done it?"

"But I haven't taken any pills for several years."

"Mom," I asked, "do you think they might be Siamese twins?"

"My God, I hope not."

Now she started reading books about twins. After the first shock, she became cheerful again.

"I think," Mom said, "what I'd really prefer is a set of fraternal twins—a boy and a girl. Of course, I'm sure we'll love them whatever they are."

Dad was silent. I knew he wasn't happy at all about the idea of twins, and that made me feel good.

"But there are problems with identical twins. People always think of them together, and if one achieves more than the other, it's a double failure for the one who isn't doing so well."

"Peter and Frank Burns are identical twins," I told her, "but both of them are dumb so nobody has to feel bad."

"There were the Henry twins when I went to school," Mom said thoughtfully. "Carol was just a little better-looking than Cathy, a little more popular, a little better in her studies . . ." Mom's voice faded away. She was off and dreaming again.

"So what happened, Mom?"

"Happened?"

"To Carol and Cathy?"

"Oh, I don't know. I didn't keep in touch after we graduated from high school. But I do think if we end up with identical twins we should make every effort to treat them as separate individuals. I will certainly never dress them in the same outfits, and I will make sure when they go to school that they're in separate classes. Don't you agree, Charlie? Charlie?"

By the end of her fifth month, Mom was so big that Dad said her belly came into the room about ten minutes before the rest of her. He was beginning to grow cheerful again. My mother, on the other hand, was becoming less cheerful. That was always the great thing about my parents. In those days, it was very rare for both of them to be angry or upset at the same time. If my mother was moody or sulky, Dad usually cheered her up. Or if it was Dad, Mom would cheer him up. I was included in this too. If I was upset, one of them was usually there to make me feel better. And in those days, just having me around made them feel good.

Mom began to grow less and less cheerful. By the end of the sixth month, her back hurt her almost all of the time. Her legs and wrists were swollen, and she stopped doing the natural childbirth exercises and sitting lotus fashion.

In her seventh month, none of her maternity clothes fitted her any more. She had to open up seams, add pieces of material, and still nothing seemed big enough to cover that huge belly of hers. My poor, little mother looked completely off balance when she stood up. She looked as if she was going to topple over. In her eighth month, everything hurt her. She couldn't sit comfortably or lie down comfortably. I had to tie her shoes for her and pick up things that she dropped. She lost her appetite, suffered heartburn and indigestion, and stopped reading books about twins. She complained of being tired, of leg cramps, heartburn, and stuffed sinuses. She complained of everything, and she lost interest in babies.

There were days when she didn't even get dressed or get out of bed. Dad said what we had to concentrate on was keeping Mom's spirits up. It was only for another month, he said, and then we wouldn't have to worry about her any more. The babies would be born, and everything would be back to . . . well, everything would be fine.

Luckily, it was summertime. If Mom hadn't gotten pregnant, this was going to be our year to tour the Scandinavian countries. Naturally, we didn't do anything or go anywhere. We stayed home and concentrated on cheering Mom up.

It wasn't easy. I rubbed her back with alcohol several times a day, and Dad tried to find funny movies on TV for her to watch. By the middle of the eighth month, Mom never even went out of the house. Dad did all the cooking, and once in a while, he and I went out to dinner and a movie.

But, mostly, we stayed home. My father took out the old photograph albums of himself and Mom when they were children, when they were teen-agers, when they were going around together, when they got married, when they had me. He told lots of funny stories about how he and Mom couldn't stand each other when they first met in college. Once he got Mom to smile, but most of the time, she complained or moaned.

The babies were due on August tenth, and Mom's suitcase was all packed and ready to go by the beginning of July. On July ninth, Mom lay in bed all day, clutching her belly, and saying, "I think, maybe . . ."

But it must have been gas because nothing happened after that.

July eleventh, Mom began to cry, and said she couldn't go on another day. Dad gave me his "Operation Cheerful" look, and we both spent the evening playing Tom Lehrer records for Mom.

Early in the morning of the twelfth, Dad woke me up, smiling. "Believe it or not," he said, "I think it's finally time to go to the hospital."

I was going along too. Even though I wouldn't be allowed in the labor room or delivery room with Mom, Dad said I could sit in the waiting room, and he'd come out and keep me posted.

I jumped up, got dressed, and ran into my parents' bedroom. Mom was sitting on the bed with her shoes untied. She was smiling. I tied her shoes, and she began talking happily about how much better she was feeling already. All the way to the hospital, Mom chatted away cheerfully. "Oh, there's another contraction . . . they're about four minutes apart now . . . Oh, isn't it exciting. Just think, Dorrie darling, this time tomorrow, you'll have a brother and a sister, or maybe two sisters or two brothers. . . . Oh, isn't it wonderful!"

She wasn't in labor long. I sat in the waiting room with

fathers-to-be and grandparents-to-be. You could see that some of them thought it was kind of funny seeing a kid hanging around the waiting room in the middle of the night. But I had as much right to be there as they did. Wasn't I a sister-to-be?

Dad kept coming out of the labor room from time to time to keep me posted. "Everything's just fine. She's really cheerful now."

At 4 A.M., Dad bought me a Coke from the Coke machine, and some coffee for himself from the coffee machine. "The contractions are pretty close together now. I don't think it will be much longer."

An hour later, he stuck his head into the waiting room and said breathlessly, "I've got to rush. They're wheeling her into the delivery room. She's as cheerful as can be."

I kept standing near the nurse at the desk after that. Soon I was going to be a sister. Next time my father came out, he would have some news for me. What would it be? Two brothers? Two sisters? One of each? At that moment, I really didn't care. We had survived the last few months. We had kept Mom cheerful. The worst was over.

Was it an hour later? Or less? Dad came out and stood next to me. He didn't say anything.

"Dad?" I cried. "Dad?"

"Oh yes," he said. "Your mother's fine, and you have two brothers."

"Oh, that's OK," I said.

"And . . ." I looked up at Dad's face. He did not look cheerful. ". . . a sister."

Chapter Five

The best part of having triplets is that they don't come home right away.

Deirdre, who was the biggest, weighed four pounds. Randolph weighed three pounds eight ounces, and Raymond, three pounds six ounces. They were the tiniest babies in the nursery and, I thought, the ugliest. Deirdre's nose spread all over her face, and the three of them were red and sort of chewed-up looking. They had no hair and looked like smooth little red rats.

my sister and brothers

Deirdre
4 lbs.

Randolpn
3 lbs. 80z

Raymond
3 lbs. 60z

The hospital was excited since it was the first set of triplets ever born there. A reporter from the San Francisco *Chronicle* came out to take pictures. He asked me what I thought of having two brothers and one sister, and I said three times as bad as having just one brother or sister. He thought it was very funny and quoted it in the article.

A man from the Baby Bye diaper service came to see Mom, and said congratulations and that the company would like to offer Mom a year's free diaper service. But other than that, nothing really good happened.

"Unfortunately," said Dr. Walker, "multiple births are so much more common nowadays that you really can't get very much with triplets. Now if you'd had sextuplets or even quintuplets, undoubtedly your whole hospital bill would be paid, all the baby food companies would offer you free food, and there would probably be some fund or other set up just for the babies. You might have gotten a house out of it. But triplets—well—you can't expect anything with just triplets."

Dad wanted to know how come Dr. Walker hadn't realized Mom was carrying triplets instead of twins. Dr. Walker explained that he had heard only two heartbeats, which meant that probably one baby was in back of the others, and that he understood from a friend who had once delivered quadruplets that the same thing had happened there.

Dad acted as if he thought Dr. Walker was somehow responsible for the triplets being born.

"But what difference would it have made even if Dr. Walker had known Mom was having triplets?" I asked him. "She still would have ended up with three babies."

He knew I was right, but he still grumbled that Dr. Walker was incompetent.

Mom was feeling good. Dad sneaked me onto her floor the next day, and there she was, walking slowly down the corridor on her way to the nursery. I had begun to think of her as always having that mountain of a belly, and it was almost a shock to see her trim and dainty again.

"Oh, it's so good to feel human again," she said, hugging and kissing me. "I can actually walk without feeling I'm going to topple over."

Everybody in the hospital was making a big fuss over her, and she loved it. Different young interns and residents kept coming in to talk to her, and, "This one doctor who was in this morning told me he and his wife have been trying to have a baby for four years with no luck. He wanted to know," Mom giggled, "if we thought yoga might help."

"Very funny!" Dad said.

"Oh, Charlie," said Mom, "I know it's a blow, but just think how much we wanted children all those years, how we tried everything, pills and diets and prayer . . ."

"Prayer?" said Dad. "You never told me you were *praying*."

"I wasn't praying for triplets, Charlie, but maybe it's the best thing that could have happened. Now we're really a big family. It's sudden, I know, but there are three of us, right, one for each of the babies. You'll see, it's going to be fun."

"Mom," I said, "which baby can I have to look after?"

"Why, any one you like. I guess you want Deirdre."

"No, her nose is too big. I think I'll take Randolph."

Randolph and Raymond were identical twins, which meant that they grew out of one egg cell and were exactly the same. The way they could tell that Raymond and Randolph were identical is that both shared only one placenta, the membrane that fed the babies inside the uterus. Deirdre is a fraternal twin to Randolph and Raymond, which means that she grew out of a different egg cell and had a placenta all to herself. Maybe that's why she was a little bigger than the boys, who must have been squished since they had to share everything between them.

Naturally, we were going to need another crib and more baby clothes. But we were lucky. The babies didn't start coming home until a month after Mom returned from the hospital. We had plenty of time to shop and rearrange the whole apartment. The living room was now the babies' room, with the three cribs lined up against the back wall. We kept most of the supplies in the dressing room and most of the babies' clothes. There were mountains of diapers and rows and rows of bottles.

"We're going to have to move," Dad said, "and right away. I ought to start looking for a big flat." Mom said she thought they ought to look for a house since she felt it was very important that each child have his and her own bedroom, which meant a five-bedroom house, and she imagined three baths and a large, sunny yard with maybe a playroom in the basement.

"Do you know how much a place like that would cost?" Dad asked.

"No," Mom admitted.

"A lot more than we can afford—especially in a neighborhood like this. I hate to upset you, Maureen, but we are not exactly rolling in money these days. You know we never saved much, and now the hospital bill alone is going to be colossal."

Mom said she had a feeling they'd find a place, but for the next few weeks, she really didn't want to be worrying about houses.

"You're right," said Dad. "Eat, drink and be merry . . ."

He didn't finish the quote which goes on to say ". . . for tomorrow we may die."

We had a few weeks then before the babies came home, and it was almost like old times. We saw a summer-stock production of *Julius Caesar*, and had dinner at Ondine's. To celebrate, Mom said. Dad didn't say anything. All sorts of presents from our friends and relatives began arriving. People knew about the triplets even though we hadn't sent out any announcements. Obviously, we couldn't use the one Mom and I had made, and my parents felt embarrassed about people thinking we were expecting them to give three baby presents. But we got lots of presents anyway—three little silver spoons from the staff at Dad's school and three stuffed Winnie-the-Pooh bears from Mom's. There were blankets, crawlers, pink and blue crib sheets, sweaters, caps, booties, a music box that played Brahms's "Lullaby" and a pair of ear plugs. Most of our relatives sent cash, and Aunt Kate promised to come out after school started.

The first baby to come home was Deirdre. She was just

Some of the presents for my sister & brothers

spoons   winnies   blankets

sweaters   EAR PLUGS   Hats

about five pounds now, but her nose still spread all over her face. Mom and I went to get her one morning. I came upstairs with Mom, and waited while she cooed a little bit over Raymond and Randolph. Then they brought Deirdre out, and Mom dressed her in a tiny, white nightgown, put a pink sweater and cap on her, and wrapped her in a pink blanket. Mom kept saying, "Oh, look how darling! How sweet!" every time Deirdre moved a fist or crossed an eye. But, honestly, I thought she was the ugliest one of the three babies and was too sorry for her to feel jealous when Mom held her close and kissed her little cheek.

I held her in the car and felt disappointed. Even though she was so small, my arm began to get tired. I tried leaning her on my lap, but her head snapped back, and Mom said I had to support her head. She stopped the car, laid Deirdre in my lap, and showed me how to crook my arm so that I kept her head from snapping. After a while my arm got tired again, and Mom had to stop the car, and turn Deirdre around the other way. We got home all right, but I was glad when Mom took her out of my arms.

Deirdre slept all the way home. Her skin was redder than the pink of her cap and sweater. I noticed that there were raised welts across her cheek and the bridge of her big, fat nose. She was still asleep when we brought her upstairs, unwrapped her from her blanket, unpeeled her cap and sweater, and put her into her crib. Mom laid her down on her stomach, and covered her with a light, white blanket with pink and blue rabbits. Then both of us stood over the crib and looked. Mom was beaming.

"Well," she said, "I have a feeling that this is going to be a lot easier than we thought. Your father is really in for a big, happy surprise."

Deirdre slept all the time. Even when she was feeding, she had a hard time keeping her eyes open. Nothing seemed to bother her, and after a few days, the welts across her cheeks and nose began to fade away. I fed her a couple of times, but it got boring. She'd keep falling asleep, and you'd have to wiggle her toes to wake her up. But Dad enjoyed feeding her. He and Mom took turns.

"Look, Charlie, how cute she is. Look, look, how she's trying to focus her eyes."

Dad held her up against his shoulder and sang to her while he burped her.

> "Oh, the music goes 'round and 'round,
> O, O, O, O, O, O,
> And it comes out here."

"Do you hear that song, Dorrie? I used to sing that to you when you were a baby."

"It's a dumb song," I told him. I didn't really think it was a dumb song but I didn't like it that he sang the same song to Deirdre that he sang to me.

The next week, Randolph came home. He was quiet in the hospital, but I noticed as I held him in the car that his eyes were open, and he kept wrinkling his face as if something smelled bad. He was much better-looking than Deirdre. His skin was white and smooth, and his nose was like a tiny knob in the middle of his face. Not that he was good-looking, but he wasn't ugly like Deirdre.

Mom said once the babies put on a little weight, she guessed they'd all be good-looking. Even I was funny-looking at first, she said, but that after a few weeks, when I filled out a little, I really was beautiful.

She let me unwrap Randolph since he was supposed to be my baby, but by the end of the evening, I had resigned from the job. It wasn't that taking care of babies is boring—I'd learned that with Deirdre—but it developed that Randolph was a screamer. He hardly slept. As soon as I put him in his crib next to Deirdre who, naturally, slept though his homecoming, he began yelling.

"He's probably hungry," Mom said, bustling around in the kitchen. She fixed him a bottle, and I sat in the rocker and tried to feed him. He was hungry all right and started sucking away. He'd take three or four big sucks, stop to yell, take three or four more sucks, stop to yell again, and so on. Finally he finished his bottle and fell asleep, but when I laid him down in his crib, he woke up and started screaming again. Finally, Mom picked him up, wrapped him in a blue blanket with white ducks, and rocked him in her arms in the rocking chair.

"Poor little baby," she said. "He hasn't been held and cuddled, and that's really what he needs. Just a little loving."

But Randolph needed more than just a little loving because he kept yelling throughout most of the night, and the next day and night, and the day and night after that.

Raymond came home three days later and was welcomed by Randolph's screams. Deirdre didn't wake up. Fortunately, it was still the summer, and all of us were home because for a while it looked as if Raymond would not only look like Randolph, but behave like him as well.

"Here," said my father, sounding like a traffic cop, "I'll feed Raymond, and, Dorrie, maybe you could just take Randolph out of here. I don't know where. Just get him out of here until Raymond falls asleep. And watch out there, Maureen, you just dropped Raymond's blanket—and while you're at it, why don't you change Dorrie, I mean Deirdre—see, she's up and beginning to cry. Or maybe I should change Deirdre, and you should feed Raymond."

It turned out that Raymond was the hungriest of all the

babies. He was up about every hour and a half yelling for his bottle. But in between bottles, Raymond slept while Randolph could sometimes hold out maybe three hours between feedings, but never seemed to stop yelling. Deirdre

did very little yelling. She had started sleeping four or five hours at a stretch at night, and my parents decided finally to move her crib into their bedroom, so that the boys wouldn't disturb her with all their drinking and noisemaking.

But it was babies all over the place. Day and night—it was bottles being washed, formulas mixed, diapers changed, laundries washed. There was nothing else but babies.

Labor Day weekend we spent taking care of babies. The year before we had gone sailing with friends of my parents who had a boat in Sausalito. We had stretched out in the sun, and eaten steaks and corn and watermelon.

"All we ever do is take care of babies," I told them. "This is Labor Day weekend, and I'm not having fun. You're supposed to have fun on Labor Day weekend."

Mom was feeding Raymond, and Dad was changing the sheet in Randolph's crib. Randolph had just chucked up part of his last bottle, and the whole room smelled of sour baby.

"Why don't you do something with Lisa today?" Mom suggested. She shifted Raymond onto her shoulder and began thumping him between his shoulders.

"Lisa went on a picnic *with her parents* to Stinson Beach."

"Well, why don't you go to a movie with Debbie? If you

like, you can have lunch at the Doggie Diner. I'll treat the two of you."

"Debbie just went to the movies last night with her *mother*. Why can't you do something with me, Mom?"

"That's not a bad idea," Dad said, putting Randolph back in his crib. Randolph began screaming, so Dad turned him over on his back and jiggled the red bells that hung over the crib. Randolph shut up for a little while, his eyes trying to focus on the bells.

"Go ahead, Maureen, you never get a chance to go out. Why don't you take a walk in the park, or go to a movie? It will do you good. Go ahead. I'll manage fine."

Randolph stopped watching the bells and started screaming. "Now, you know you can't manage by yourself," Mom said. "At least I have Mrs. Olsen most of the time when you're not here, and, oh, I didn't have a chance to tell you, but Mrs. Olsen won't be able to come in and work for us any more after next week. She says she's having trouble with her varicose veins and thinks she needs to be off her feet for a while."

"But, Mom," I said, "can't you come out even for a little walk?"

"Oh, Dorrie, I'd love to," Mom said, "but I just can't right now. I know it's been hard for you but just be patient, darling. You'll see in a few months, life will be so much easier. Anyway, I have an idea. Why don't you and Dad take a walk over to Baskin-Robbins and get some ice cream. You can bring me back a jamoca almond fudge sugar cone, and pick up some Similac at the drugstore. Maybe tonight, if we can get all the babies down, we'll play Monopoly or Scrabble, or whatever you like. You'll see, we'll have lots of fun."

My father and I took a walk to Baskin-Robbins, and picked up some Similac, and came home. Maybe we had been gone an hour or so, but we could hear them yelling as we came up the stairs—the three of them—Raymond, Randolph, and Mom.

65

They were all in the living room, and on the gold oak dining-room table was a mountain of laundry that Mom had been trying to fold. There were diapers and blankets all over the furniture. Mom was holding Raymond in her lap, the two of them sobbing together while Randolph was kicking his feet and screaming his head off in his crib. And faintly, from the dressing room, came the little, mewing cries of Deirdre.

Dad handed Mom the jamoca almond fudge cone and went off to get Deirdre. I took Raymond away from her, and held him while she began licking at her cone, the tears pouring down her cheeks. After a while she lay down for a nap and slept all through the evening. Dad was too busy to play Monopoly with me, and I went to bed early.

That was the first Labor Day weekend that I did not have any fun at all.

Chapter Six

Day and night the babies had to be fed, washed, changed, dressed, held, and heard. There was no corner of any room where you could escape from them. Everywhere were mounds of baby clothes, blankets, and diapers, and the kitchen was filled with drying and half-washed bottles. The doctor decided that Randolph needed to be put on a special formula, and his bottles and nipples had to be sterilized. It didn't help any, and as the weeks passed, the doctor kept changing Randolph's formula. Sometimes my parents would get mixed up, and feed Randolph's formula to Raymond, and once Dad fed Raymond twice and missed Randolph altogether.

Both of my parents were groggy from lack of sleep. Occasionally, I'd hear them at night and get up. But, generally, I slept through the night. From the start, Mom said she didn't want me to lose any sleep. She also said that she wanted me to go on doing whatever I had been doing before the triplets were born. Which was impossible since what I had been doing was enjoying myself *alone* with Mom and Dad. But once the babies were born both of them were too busy to have any time left over for me. Dad never made Caesar salads any more, and Mom stopped cooking.

"TV dinners again tonight?" I complained.

"This kind is not really bad," Mom said. "See, it's from a recipe they use in the Casa Blanca, and it's a special enchilado-taco combination with refried beans on the side."

"It looks icky to me."

"Oh, stop your whining and eat," Dad grumbled. "It's nearly time for the six-o'clock feeding. There goes Randolph, or is it Raymond this time?"

That was another thing—suddenly my parents were arguing—with each other and with me.

"Why don't you go and lie down for a nap, Charlie? I can manage."

"No—why don't you take a nap?"

"I don't want a nap. I can't sleep anyway. You go. You need it."

"What do you mean, I need it."

"Well, you do, don't you?"

"No, but you meant something else. What did you mean?"

"I just think you need a nap. You're tired, and you're . . ."

"What?"

"Well, you're not exactly lovable, are you?"

"What do you mean I'm not exactly lovable?"

"Look, Charlie, don't take a nap if you don't want to. Just get out of my way and let me get some work done."

"Oh? And I haven't been doing any work, is that what you mean? All morning, giving them baths, and folding the laundry, and . . ."

"Go away!" screamed my mother. "Go away!"

"With pleasure," yelled my father, storming out of the

house. But fifteen minutes later he was back because he knew the six-o'clock feeding was coming up.

Everything got worse when school started. Mrs. Olsen, our cleaning lady left, and Mom hired another woman, Mrs. Mellon, who came for two days and never returned. Then the agency sent a young woman named Mary Ellen Wood who lasted a week before Mom fired her because she kept breaking things and dropped Deirdre once from the dressing table. Nothing seemed to work out. Either we'd get somebody who was good and quit, or we'd get somebody horrible whom Mom had to fire. In between housekeepers and after school, Mom began to make more and more demands on me. I didn't like it.

"Here now, Dorrie, you're just going to have to feed Raymond while I take care of Randolph. Whoever finishes first can feed Deirdre."

"In a few minutes, Mom, as soon as I finish this chapter."

"Right now, Dorrie, you can read later."

"I never get a chance to read, Mom, and you said you wanted me to keep on doing whatever I was doing before they were born, but every time I open a book lately you keep finding things for me to do, and . . ."

"DORRIE, GET OVER HERE AND TAKE THIS BABY RIGHT NOW!"

Our beautiful, glamorous apartment was suddenly crowded and uncomfortable. At night, after dinner, we couldn't sit in the living room because the babies were sleeping there. So we stayed in the kitchen, folding laundry, washing bottles, and arguing. When my friends came over, we had to stay in my bedroom in case the babies were napping. Mom wore old jeans all the time and blouses that were always spotted with chucked-up milk stains. There was a clutter of baby things everywhere. All the furniture was draped with blankets, sweaters, and crawlers. You couldn't open a closet without being hit by a stuffed animal.

"It's just horrible," I told Mom. "It's like being drowned in babies."

"Yes, but it's all going to be worth it," she said. "Raymond is really putting on weight now, and I don't think Randolph is yelling quite so much. And just see how Deirdre smiles. She really has a wonderful disposition. A few more months and the worst will really be over. Just be patient."

Dad said that the worst problem was the apartment. As soon as we found a larger place he was sure that everything would be much easier. Sundays, he tried to spend house hunting, but it was hard to get away even for a few hours because he was needed to help with the babies. And then, everything was so expensive, he didn't see how he could ever find the kind of house Mom wanted for the kind of price we could afford to pay.

One Sunday afternoon in late September, between the two-o'clock and the six-o'clock feeding, Dad and I went out to check on an ad in the paper. It said: "Spacious 4 brs. 2 ba. lg. yd. good for handyman. A steal at this price."

"Do you consider yourself a handyman?" I asked Dad as we were driving.

"That just means that the place needs repairs," he said, reaching over and turning off the radio which I had just turned on.

"Dad," I continued, "if this place has four bedrooms, that's not going to be enough. You and Mom need one bedroom, I need one, and if each baby gets one that means we're one short. And Mom says she wants each of us to have our own bedroom, and . . ."

"Let's just wait and see, Dorrie."

"Fine with me, Dad, but it still is going to be one bedroom short."

"Mmm."

"Dad."

"What?"

"Did you know that there is almost 100 per cent chance of Raymond being mentally ill if Randolph is?"

"No, I didn't," said my father, "but I'm beginning to think that my chances look pretty good too."

71

"But seriously, Dad, I just read that in a twin book. They had a chart and it's just about positive that if one identical twin becomes mentally ill the other one will too. The same is true of criminal tendencies. So if Raymond becomes a criminal, chances are that Randolph will be too—but it's different for Deirdre. Even though both Raymond and Randolph become murderers, it's not necessarily true that she would be one too. But with identical twins, and this is really interesting, Dad, even if we separated them and, say, sent Randolph to China and Raymond to France, it would make no difference."

Dad switched on the radio, and we listened to the weather forecast until we arrived at the house.

It was a mess. All the rooms needed painting inside, and the steps were cracked and sagging on the outside. One of the bathrooms had a toilet that didn't flush, and the other bathroom had barfy yellow and wine-colored tile. The kitchen was old and crumbly, and led out to a landing that overlooked a yard that was large and sunny, as the ad said. But it was also on a slant and choked with weeds. I walked down a rickety pair of steps into the yard and thought to myself how lucky I was to live where I did.

Somebody was looking at me out of the back window of the next house. It was a girl, an unfriendly-looking girl. She opened the window and shouted, "Hey, you—are you buying the Leonards' house?"

"No."

"You better not because it's haunted."

"What do you mean?"

"The old man died there a couple of months ago, and I think his wife murdered him."

"That doesn't mean it's haunted."

"What do you know, stupid! It's haunted all right, and somebody is buried in the yard right about where you're standing."

I ran back up the rickety steps and found Dad talking to the agent.

"mean-faced girl"

"Dad," I said, "there's somebody buried in the yard."
The agent laughed. So did Dad.

"And an old man was murdered here a couple of months ago. Come on, Dad, let's go home. This place is creepy."

Dad really looked cheerful when we got back into the car and started driving home. "What a place!" he said.

"Isn't it?" I agreed.

Both of us laughed.

"And they'll come down," Dad continued. "It was great how you brought up that nonsense about somebody being murdered and buried in the yard. Did you see the look on the agent's face?"

"No, it was two people—one was murdered, and another one was buried in the yard."

"Well, however it was, I think we can really get them down three or four thousand."

"What do you mean, Dad? You don't like it, do you? It's a horrible place."

"Oh, it'll be great when we're finished with it, Dorrie. It's a real Victorian. Did you notice the wooden doorknobs and that fantastic fixture in the hall?"

"No, I didn't, but the whole place is dirty and disgusting.

73

There aren't any beautiful views from any of the windows, and this mean-looking girl lives next door. I hate it, Dad, I hate it!"

Our neighbor, Mrs. Coombs, stayed with me and the triplets so that Mom could go back with Dad and look at the house.

That night, I had my first real blow-up. "You promised!" I kept screaming to Mom. "You promised that we'd never move unless I liked the place as much as I like this one. You promised, Mom, you promised!"

"Yes, I know I did," Mom said, "but you have to be fair, Dorrie. When I promised I thought we were only going to have one baby. I didn't know we'd have triplets."

"*We* didn't have triplets," I screamed. "*You* did. Don't blame it on me. It wasn't my fault—and I didn't want them. I didn't even want one triplet. But you promised, Mom, and if you don't keep your promise then you're a liar."

"Dorrie," Mom said, "don't you understand? We just have no choice. We can't stay here, and anything larger in this area would be more than we can afford."

"You don't even care about me any more," I shouted. "It's like I don't even exist!"

"Now, Dorrie," Mom said, trying to pull me over to her, "that place will really be lovely once we get it fixed. We'll clean it up and have it painted before we move in, and then, after, we'll remodel the kitchen, put a deck outside, and plant flowers in the yard. You know how Dad and I always like to work over old things and make them lovely. It's really a nice, old house with good lines . . ."

"No, it isn't," I yelled. "It's just an old house, an old, ugly house—and I won't move there. I won't, I won't, I WON'T!"

Chapter Seven

By the end of October we were in.

Everybody knows those stories about families who buy old ratty houses, and spend a little bit of money, and maybe a little more time and work, and before you know it, the old ratty house turns into a real palace. Well, our house was an old ratty place when we bought it, is still an old ratty place, and no amount of time, effort, or money can turn it into anything else.

The place *was* painted before we moved in, and all the downstairs floors were scraped and finished. The toilet that didn't flush was repaired, and the flue in the living room fireplace was cleaned out. Dad had the outside stairs repaired, but by that time there wasn't any money left to paint the outside of the house which was sort of a pale, liver brown.

Dad kept talking about the wooden doorknobs and the glass fixture in the hall, and Mom kept saying that the built-in cupboard in the dining room had real charm and that there was a fantastic view of the Golden Gate Bridge from the upstairs bathroom (if you stuck your head out of the window). But the truth of the matter was that all the rooms were much smaller than the rooms in our old place and that the dining room, kitchen, and two of the bedrooms were dark and looked out on alleys.

The first night in the new house was a horror. We sat around our pretty oak table in the small, dark kitchen with its view of our neighbor's bathroom window. Dad had picked up some Kentucky Fried Chicken but he was the only one eating. I was crying, and Mom was moving her fork through a cardboard container of french fries and trying not to notice me.

"First thing," she said thoughtfully, looking away from me and at the kitchen window, "I think I'll put up some rice paper over the glass. That way, we'll still get the light but we'll also have more privacy."

Our neighbors' bathroom window had opened by this time, and the mean-looking girl and a younger child were standing there watching us.

"Do you think you ought to do that right away?" Dad whispered, nodding pleasantly at the two spectators. "I mean, our neighbors might get the impression that we're not very friendly."

Mom picked up a shriveled french fry, held it in front of her nose, but didn't allow it to go any further. "Well," she said, "maybe you're right. I could put up some curtains, I suppose."

"Maybe that would be better." He turned and smiled at me. "I think I'm going to get started on the yard—and pull up all those weeds. What do you say, Dorrie? How about you and me getting out sometime soon and doing a little restoring. Maybe we'll find a marble faun under all that underbrush."

"You'll probably find the Sleeping Beauty," I said bitterly, the tears rolling down my cheeks. "I told you there's somebody buried out there."

"Oh, Dorrie," Mom laughed, putting the french fry back into the container. "That's just one of those charming stories that surround all old houses. Why don't you have something to eat, and get to bed early? By tomorrow you'll see, everything will look much brighter."

Brighter was the wrong word because my bedroom was one of the dark rooms, and in the morning, I awoke to a dismal, gray light that reminded me to start crying again. The only pleasant part of the day was showing my parents how miserable I was. Whenever they spoke to me or looked at me, I was crying. It was the longest cry of my life—lasting from Friday night when we moved in through Saturday night when Dad went out for pizza, and I stopped crying briefly to eat, through Sunday night when I went to bed exhausted.

Monday morning, my eyes were so swollen and red that Mom, I think, would have been willing to let me stay home from school and keep crying.

Dad said no. "You've broken all records," he said, "but today you're going to school—wet or dry—you can decide."

"What is it, darling?" Mom asked gently. "Are you worried about the new school?"

Of course I wasn't at all worried about the new school. I was pretty sure that wherever I went to school I was bound to be the top student and have all the teachers crazy about me. But I wasn't about to give up any weapons that were available to me.

"Yes," I wept, "I'm worried about the new school. I don't know any of the teachers or any of the kids, and I'm scared, I'm scared. I hate it here. I want to go home."

I laid my head down on the table, and sobbed.

"Charles—really, she's in no condition."

"Maureen," thundered my father, "she is going to school today if I have to carry her there!"

Randolph began yelling.

"Now see what you've done!" shouted my mother. "You woke Randolph up, and I just got him down."

"I wish I was dead," I cried.

"Now listen, Dorrie," my father whispered. "Enough is enough. You've been sorry for yourself for a whole weekend—that should last you for a couple of months at least. Today you're going to school. Go upstairs, get yourself dressed, and be down here in ten minutes. Do you hear?"

"I can't, I can't," I wept and moved my head around on my arm so that I could see my mother out of one wet eye.

Randolph was really screaming now, and slowly you could hear the answering call of Raymond. Randolph had a bedroom all to himself while Raymond and Deirdre shared one. My parents felt that if Randolph was by himself, his screaming might not disturb the other two. But, as I understood from my reading, his screaming might not disturb Deirdre, but Raymond, being identical, couldn't help being affected. Experts did not entirely agree, but it seemed very likely that identical twins were on the same wave length with each other and experienced a mysterious bond unknown to other siblings. There had been cases reported of twins dying at the same time even though they were apart, twins experiencing pain together even though only one was hurt, and twins generally responding to each other's needs. But this was not the time to explain all this to my parents who had lost all intellectual curiosity anyway.

My mother took a deep breath, wrinkled her face, and looked as if she was going to burst into tears herself. I wept louder, hoping to encourage her. But my father stood up suddenly, picked me up, and carried me over to the stairs.

"Dorrie," he said, "I want you to go upstairs, and get dressed RIGHT NOW! Do you understand?"

I slammed the door to my bedroom as hard as I could, and was pleased to hear Deirdre join the chorus.

School was boring. Nothing bad happened to me, and nothing good either. The teachers were pleasant, the kids weren't particularly mean, but nobody noticed me as me. I was just the new girl that had to be introduced to different teachers and shown where the lockers and the lunchroom were.

Later in the day, somebody did notice me. It was while I was walking home from school that the mean-faced girl in the next house caught up with me. She was about a head taller than me, and her hair wasn't combed. It hung in dirty curls around her face, and there was a big grease stain on her sweater.

"You," she said, "what's your name?"

"Dorrie."

"Dorrie What?"

"Dorrie O'Brien."

"You Jewish?"

I burst out laughing, and she stepped on my foot, called me a fat slob, and ran off.

So, naturally, I was crying when I got home, but Mom didn't even notice that I was until I stood right in front of her and let a few tears drip into her lap, which contained Deirdre and some diapers she was folding.

"Darling, how was school?"

"Horrible. I hate my teachers. I hate the kids. The food is lousy, and that big bully next door picked on me and called me names, and if we don't get out of here right away, I'll run away or I'll kill myself."

"Poor baby!" Mom said cheerfully. I couldn't help noticing how cheerful she sounded, and it didn't help. "How about some milk and cookies?"

It would have been more dignified if I could have said no, I wasn't hungry, but unfortunately I'm always hungry, even when I'm miserable. So I stood there crying, but not saying no to the milk and cookies.

"Here, darling, sit down, and I'll bring us both a snack. Why don't you hold Deirdre, and maybe fold a few diapers while I'm gone."

Deirdre wiggled in my lap. She arched her back, waved her arms around, and laughed up at me. Her nose no longer spread all over her face, her skin was smooth and white, and her hair was coming in bright red. She was beautiful, and that made me feel more miserable. I cried, and she laughed, until Mom returned with a tray of milk and graham crackers.

"Don't we have anything better than graham crackers?" I wept.

"I'm afraid not, Dorrie. I haven't shopped for days, but this afternoon when Mrs. Cole comes back, I'll get out and

79

pick up a load of groceries. You can come with me if you like."

"Who's Mrs. Cole?"

Mom looked so cheerful that I cried a little harder. "Oh, Dorrie, I just can't believe how everything seems to be perfect all of a sudden. You know how I kept trying to find somebody to help me take care of the babies, and how nobody seemed right. Well, this morning, I was really feeling down. Raymond had diarrhea for the second day, and Randolph was screaming as usual, and I burned my hand on the coffeepot, and there was a blister under my thumb that was so painful I couldn't even hold anything. In the middle of all this, the doorbell suddenly rang, and there was Mrs. Cole. She lives across the street in that green and white house, and she just dropped by to say hello."

"So?" The graham crackers were limp and did not crunch when you bit into them.

"Well, she has six kids of her own, all of them in school. Her youngest is your age, and his name is Michael. Did you run across him at school? Michael Cole?"

"No, and if I did, I wouldn't have noticed anyway. Because I hated school, and I'm so miserable here, I . . ."

"Well," said my mother, "so Mrs. Cole looked at the triplets, and thought they were all beautiful—especially Deirdre." Mom was holding Deirdre now, and she took a few seconds to go "goo" and "ga" to her while Deirdre rolled around wriggling and laughing.

"These graham crackers are stale," I said, the tears falling into my milk.

"Anyway," continued my mother, "Mrs. Cole had a set of twins—they're thirteen years old—incidentally, all her children are boys, so you can imagine how she really fussed over Deirdre. But she told me how hard it was when all her children were little, and how much time she has now, and how she misses having babies around. So one thing led to another, and oh, Dorrie, isn't it wonderful—she's agreed to work for me. She's so warm and good. You can see the way she cuddles the babies and talks to them—even Randolph smiled at her. She says she'll even baby sit for me at night if I need her, and if she can't, then her oldest boy, Victor, who's eighteen, can. I'm so happy, Dorrie, I just can't believe how everything's working out for us."

"Not for us," I told her. "Nothing's working out for me."

"Oh, that's right," my mom said, trying not to look so cheerful. "You had a hard day at school, didn't you? Well, why don't you tell me about it, and . . ."

But just then the doorbell rang, and Mom had to get up to answer it. Mrs. Cole had returned with her identical twins, Robert and Richard. Mom made a big fuss over them even though I thought they were fat, dumb-looking boys. The only interesting thing about them was that they were mirror-image twins. Robert was right-handed and Richard was left-handed.

Robert had a mole on the right side of his nose, and Richard on the left. There was another neighbor with her too, Mrs. Wong, and three of her kids.

In the course of all the introductions, Mom finally got around to me.

"So this is Dorrie," said Mrs. Cole. She put an arm around

81

my shoulder and gave me a little squeeze. "How lucky you are, Mrs. O'Brien, to have two daughters—and two beautiful ones at that."

It was when Mrs. Cole said "two daughters" that I probably experienced the worst moment in my entire life. Naturally, once the triplets were born, I realized that they were my parents' children too, but somehow until Mrs. Cole said "two daughters" I hadn't realized that not only was I no longer an only child, I was also no longer an only daughter. And that business of "two beautiful daughters" was just politeness on Mrs. Cole's part. I wasn't beautiful. I'd never be beautiful. But Deirdre at three and a half months was already beautiful. By the time she was eleven, my age now, I'd be twenty-two, grown-up, and maybe even gone from the house. It was like being dead, and my parents having Deirdre, beautiful Deirdre, and her brothers to make them happy.

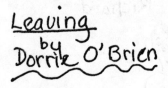

Leaving
by Dorrie O'Brien

① Dorrie has an idea! ② SHE takes $12 out of her desk and $168 out of the bank

"Excuse me," I said, and ran upstairs to my room. I could hear the talk and the laughter moving into the kitchen. The sound of Mom putting up a kettle of water for tea, chairs being scraped, a child crying. What was I doing here in the middle of all these noisy people who didn't care at all about me?

I thought about running away. There was twelve dollars in my desk, and one hundred and sixty-eight dollars in my bank account. I had the pass book for it and could make deposits and withdrawals by myself. If I took the money out of the bank, and added the twelve dollars to it, that would give me one hundred and eighty dollars. I wouldn't need to take much in the way of clothes. I really began warming to the subject. Maybe I could run away tomorrow after school—or maybe before school. Why wait, as a matter of fact? Why not right now? Well, the bank wasn't open this late, so it had better be in the morning. I could make believe I had my books in my knapsack but I'd really have the clothes and things I needed to run away. But instead of going to school, I'd head for the bank and wait for it to open. Once I had the money, I could go . . . go . . .

That's where the whole idea folded. Go? Where? I couldn't go to my grandparents. I only have one set left anyway, on Mom's side, and they're in a home for old people. I couldn't go there. It wouldn't be any fun living with Aunt Kate or with any of Dad's brothers except for Uncle Jim. He's got a daughter, Sharon, just my age, and pretty nice, and a little boy named Jeffrey who's quiet and doesn't bother anybody. But Uncle Jim is a colonel in the Army, and he and his family are in Germany now. My money would never get me that far. So where else could I go?

Maybe I could hide out in a museum like the kids in that book I read, or even in Macy's. But it seemed to me that the museum or Macy's might feel kind of spooky at night, especially if you were all alone. I tried to think of different grownups who might like me enough to take me into their lives, but I couldn't think of a single one.

Trapped, that's what I was—trapped. Nothing could be worse. Suddenly my door opened. One of the little Wong kids stood there, watching me. She was about two and a half and had a couple of graham crackers in her hand. There were crumbs on her face, crumbs on her shirt, and in a second, a clump of crumbs on my floor.

"What do you want?" I asked.

She didn't say anything, just watched me solemnly, standing motionless at the door.

"Look, I'm busy now. Why don't you go find your mother?"

I got up, moved toward her, and she suddenly held up her hand, and offered me the damp, limp graham cracker. "Gooky," she said.

"No thanks," I told her. "Now I'll show you where the staircase is, and you go back downstairs like a good, little girl."

"No!" she yelled, and moved past me into my room. She dropped the cracker on the floor, and stood looking up at my shelf of foreign dolls. "Dolly," she said, pointing. "Dolly."

"Yes, they're dollies, but you can't touch them. Here, I'll take you back to your mother." I bent down, and tried to pick her up, but she sat down suddenly on the floor and began howling.

In two years' time, Deirdre and Randolph and Raymond would be like this child. They would come into my room, mess it up with graham cracker crumbs, want to play with all my things, and refuse to leave when I asked them.

No, I realized, this was not the worst time in my life. That was yet to come.

Chapter Eight

You never really know how bad things can get until they get worse. The first few months of the triplets were bad, but at least all three of us—my mother, my father, and myself—were miserable together. But later, after Mrs. Cole came, my father and mother stopped being so miserable. Then I was miserable all by myself, and nothing is as bad as that.

Mrs. Cole came every day during the week to help Mom. Sometimes she even came on the weekends. If she wasn't there, some other member of the Cole family was. Mrs. Wong started dropping in, and so did two other neighbors, Mrs. Kadri and Mrs. Esposito.

Mom said, "I never thought it would be possible to feel this way, but some days there are actually more hands than I need."

"And more mouths too," I told her. "You're never alone any more. There's always somebody here when I come home from school, somebody sitting around drinking tea and yapping about their kids. I never get a chance to talk to you alone. You've always got company."

"But we have dinner alone, and we're usually alone at night."

"Except you and Dad are always out."

"Now, Dorrie, you're exaggerating. Yesterday, Dad and I went to a P.T.A. meeting at *your* school, so it's really only that one evening last week that just . . ."

87

"Just the two of you," I suggested, "went out for dinner and a real, good time."

"Yes," said Mom, "it was a good time. But aren't you forgetting, Dorrie, that we've been out a couple of times with you too. And once in a while, we do need to be by ourselves."

"You never used to need to be by yourselves. Why, all of a sudden, do you need to be by yourselves?"

"People change, Dorrie," Mom said. "You can't always stay the same. Life wouldn't be very interesting if it was always the same."

"But sometimes," I told her, "it can change for the worse, and that's the way it is for me."

I talked a lot to Mom about how miserable I was. I talked to Dad too and to anybody who'd listen. Even Mr. Cooperstein, the counselor in school. He called me down after I'd been in school a month. "How are you getting along?" he asked me.

"Terribly," I told him.

Mr. Cooperstein laughed.

"I mean it," I told him. "I hate school. I have no friends. The girl next door picks on me, and there's nothing I can do about it. We have triplets in my house, and my mother is too busy with them or too busy yapping with the neighbors to have any time for me. My father tells me to stop whining whenever I try to talk to him. One of the babies, Randolph, cries all the time, but nobody tells him to stop whining. The girl triplet, Deirdre, was so ugly when she was born, I was actually sorry for her. But now she's beautiful. She used to have a big, fat nose in a little face, and now she has a little nose in a big, fat face. She also has red hair, big blue eyes, and a cheerful disposition. We live in an ugly house which my parents promised they would make beautiful, but they haven't, and there is somebody buried out in the yard."

Mr. Cooperstein hesitated and then asked, "What kind of marks are you getting?"

"Oh—A in everything, as usual."

"Well, that's just fine then," he told me. "And I'm sure everything *else* will work out. Just be patient."

That day, Genevieve James walked behind me all the way home from school. Genevieve James was the name of the girl next door. She walked so close to me that she kept stepping on the backs of my shoes. I ignored her. She couldn't stand it when I ignored her or laughed at her. So naturally I did one or the other, and it was only when she couldn't see that I cried.

"Marshmallow legs," she called out, referring to the color and consistency of my legs.

I kept walking.

"Hey, watch out," she yelled, "it's going to fall on you."

I walked on.

"You better turn around," she said finally, getting mad as she always did sooner or later, "or I'm going to kick you right in the butt."

So I kept walking, and she kicked me in the butt, and I looked at her as if she was the lowest insect in the world, and as soon as I got inside my house I began to cry.

For a change, it was quiet—no clinking of tea cups or ladies' voices talking all at once about their kids.

"Mom," I sobbed, "Mom."

Mrs. Cole came out of the kitchen. She pulled me close to her and pressed my head into her big front. One good thing about Mrs. Cole is her smell—like flour and raisins. Naturally, I hated her because she was responsible for making my parents feel so happy while I was so miserable. But it was nothing personal. Mrs. Cole is a very friendly, motherly person, and if I didn't know her, I would probably like her a lot.

"What is it, Dorrie?" she asked, patting my back and pushing my face deeper into her bosom.

"Where's my mother?" I cried.

"She's out shopping, but what happened? Are you all right?"

I told Mrs. Cole all about Genevieve James—how she

teases me and bothers me and never leaves me alone.

"But what do you do?" she asked.

"Nothing. I never talk to her. I never look at her. I make believe she doesn't exist."

"Poor thing," said Mrs. Cole, and I sniffed, thinking that Mrs. Cole was a very understanding person, even if I did hate her so much.

"Her mother is crazy," said Mrs. Cole. "She sleeps all day, and stays out all night, and never gives them anything decent to eat. You really should try to be a little kinder."

"WHAT?"

Mrs. Cole opened the kitchen window and yelled, "Genevieve!"

"But why should I be kinder?" I asked. "She's the one who picks on me and teases me."

"Genevieve!" Mrs. Cole yelled, a little louder. Genevieve appeared at her bathroom window, and Mrs. Cole said, "Shame on you, Genevieve."

"What for?" said Genevieve, a sulky look on her face.

"You know what for, and I don't want you to lay a hand on Dorrie ever again, do you understand?"

"I never laid a hand on her," Genevieve replied (which was true since she usually kicked me or butted me or pushed me with her elbows).

"Don't you be fresh to me, Genevieve."

Genevieve was silent, but she stood there, staring right back into Mrs. Cole's face.

"All right. Now I want you to come over here, right now."

"Me?" said Genevieve.

"Yes, we're going to have some tea and cookies, and we'll all be friends."

"Oh sure," Genevieve said, grinning. "I'm coming right over." She closed the window.

"Thanks very much," I told Mrs. Cole, "but I'm never going to be friends with that weirdo."

"Now, Dorrie," said Mrs. Cole, "if you had been friends with her right away, she never would have teased you or hurt you. She has no father and a crazy mother and that's why she's mean."

"But that's no reason for me to be friends with her. She's dirty and dumb besides being mean, and I never make friends with people like that."

"You would be mean and dirty and dumb too if you had parents like hers," Mrs. Cole said. "You should try to be a little kinder or you'll grow up to be selfish and unhappy."

"This is really crazy," I told Mrs. Cole. "You're blaming me because Genevieve is such a stinker, and you're telling me that I should make friends with people I can't stand. It doesn't make any sense at all."

The doorbell rang, and Genevieve James stood outside, smiling. Her face was dirty and so were her hands. There were black bands under each fingernail.

Genevieve

"Come in, come in, Genevieve," said Mrs. Cole, putting an arm around Genevieve's shoulder and giving her a little squeeze.

Genevieve looked at me, and her smile got bigger. There was a green film on her teeth. I looked away.

We all walked into the kitchen, and Mrs. Cole asked us if we wanted milk or tea.

"Milk," I said.

"Tea," said Genevieve.

Mrs. Cole looked at Genevieve's dirty face and at her dirty hands. "Dorrie, why don't you and Genevieve wash up since you both just came back from school. Show Genevieve where the bathroom is."

On the way, Genevieve stopped to look at the living room. "Wow," she said, "this is really gorgeous and there's the piano. I could hear it but I never knew who played. Is it you?"

"Sometimes, and sometimes my mother. Even my father can play. All of us can play in this family."

"It's gorgeous," she said, pressing a key with her dirty finger and leaving a grimy spot.

We washed up, and she left a dirty streak on the towel when she was finished. Her face and hands were clean, but there was still a dirty band under each fingernail.

We sat around the kitchen table, and Mrs. Cole and Genevieve talked. I listened except when Mrs. Cole asked me a direct question and I had to answer. Naturally, Randolph began yelling. You could always count on Randolph yelling, especially when anybody was sitting down trying to eat or drink something.

Genevieve went upstairs with Mrs. Cole to get him, and I trailed along too.

"Oh, what a gorgeous baby," Genevieve cooed. "Look at those big, blue eyes, and those blond curls, and just look how he wrinkles his nose—oh—he's just gorgeous."

Randolph

I guess Randolph was good-looking. Most of the time you were so busy noticing his yelling that you didn't notice too much else about him.

"Please, Mrs. Cole, can I hold him, please?"

"Sure, Genevieve, just pick him up carefully, and hold his head—that's right. There you go. Sit down over here."

Genevieve sat down and held Randolph stiffly for a few seconds. Naturally he began to cry.

"Oh, why is he crying?" Genevieve asked. "What am I doing wrong?"

"You're not doing anything wrong," I told her. "He always cries." I took him away from her, laid him down on the dressing table, and began changing him. Genevieve was watching me, so I held a safety pin in my mouth, and sprinkled him with powder, and let her see how experienced I was with babies. Ordinarily, I never changed any one of them unless I had to.

Randolph screamed and kicked all the time I was changing him, and Genevieve said, "What does he want? Can't you do something?"

"We'll give him a bottle as soon as I get him changed. Maybe that will shut him up."

"Can I give it to him?"

"Well, Genevieve, I don't know . . ."

"Please!"

"Of course you can," said Mrs. Cole. "Here, put this diaper on your shoulder so you can burp him, and there, Dorrie's finished, hold the baby like this, and the bottle like that, and there you go."

Randolph was hungry. He just about snapped the nipple off the bottle and began sucking hard. Great big bubbles appeared in the bottle, and Genevieve smiled and said, "Oh, he's hungry, isn't he? Am I holding it right? When should I burp him?"

I was looking at her dirty fingernails and wondering how my mother would feel about her feeding Randolph. I looked at Mrs. Cole and noticed that she was looking at Genevieve's fingernails too. If only my mom would come in, right now. Maybe she'd stop thinking Mrs. Cole was so great.

There was Mom in the doorway.

"I wondered where everybody was," she said, and looked at Genevieve.

"This is Genevieve James," I said, "the girl who . . . uh . . . the girl next door."

"Oh, yes," said Mom. "Hi, Genevieve! It looks like they've put you right to work."

"But this isn't work, Mrs. O'Brien—it's fun. He's such a gorgeous baby. I never saw a baby like this one. He really is gorgeous. Oh, I think he's smiling at me. Mrs. Cole, look, isn't he smiling?"

"It's gas," I told her.

"No, he's smiling all right," said Mrs. Cole. "And you should feel very proud, Genevieve. Randolph just does not smile for everybody."

Randolph went back to drinking, and then, I think, Mom noticed Genevieve's fingernails.

"Are you getting tired, Genevieve?" Mom asked.

"Oh no, I'm not tired. I could do this all day. I love feeding him. He's such a gor . . ."

"Yes," I said, "you told us that already."

"But he is—the most gorgeous baby I ever saw in my whole life."

"He is nice, isn't he?" Mom said, looking at Randolph as if she was seeing him for the first time. "Most people seem to think Raymond is better-looking because he's chubbier, and of course, Deirdre . . ."

But later, when Genevieve saw Raymond and Deirdre, she insisted that Randolph was not only "the most gorgeous baby of them all" but "the most gorgeous baby in the world" as well.

"Can I come back and help tomorrow?" she asked Mom. "I can take care of Randolph if he's up."

"Of course you can come," said Mom, smiling. "What a sweet child," she said after Genevieve left.

"Sweet!" I said. "She's the one who's been picking on me

94

since we moved here. And she's dirty. Did you see those fingernails? How could you let her touch Randolph, much less feed him? Yuk!"

"I'll show her how to take care of her nails tomorrow," Mom said, "and any friend of Randolph's has got to have some good qualities."

Mrs. Cole said, smiling at me, "Making friends always helps to sweeten the disposition."

"She's not going to be my friend," I said.

"She's not going to need to be your friend," said Mrs. Cole. "She has another friend in this house, and he's . . ."

"The most gorgeous baby in the world," I said, finishing the sentence for her.

Chapter Nine

Genevieve came every day after school, and for as many
hours over the weekend as my mother would allow. Mom
bought her a manicure set and taught her how to look after
her nails. She explained to Genevieve that people who handle
babies must be scrupulously clean. They must have clean
faces and hands, clean hair, and should take frequent showers.

I guess Genevieve was willing to make any kind of sacrifice
just as long as she could take care of Randolph. At first, she
would show up with her face and hands clean, but with a ring
of dirt around the clean parts. But after a while, she actually
began looking clean all over.

"There must be something about Randolph we're missing,"
Dad said, "an unseen, but not unheard, charm, I suppose."

"Genevieve is a very sweet girl," Mom said. "It's just that
she and Harold have been so terribly neglected. Mrs. Cole
says that their mother sometimes leaves them alone for days
at a time. Evidently some of the neighbors think she's not a
fit mother and that the children should be taken away."

"What happened to their father?" I asked.

"Nobody's seen him for years. It really is amazing how
unfit some people are to be parents," said my mother. "Why
have children if all you do is neglect them?"

"Yes," I said. "That's what I ask myself all the time."

"There goes our broken record," said Dad, laughing.
Lately, he and my mother had taken to laughing at me
whenever I started complaining.

"Think about Genevieve whenever you feel you're being neglected," my mother smiled. "Then you'll really know what neglected means."

"I don't have to think about Genevieve to know what neglected means," I told her. "But what would happen to them if they were taken away from their mother?"

"They would probably be put into foster homes."

"Why would anybody want to take foster kids anyway," I asked. "It must be horrible having strange kids in your house all the time, touching your things and getting in your way."

"You know what your problem is?" Dad asked.

"Yes, I know, but actually I have three problems."

"No, only one. Your problem is that you suffer from the 'Me-Mes.' It's common to only children and is seldom fatal. But it's very trying on friends and relations."

Mom said, "People take foster children for a number of reasons. The best one is that they like children and want to see them happy. Some families take foster children because they want companions for their own children, and some because they think they can make something out of the money the agency allows them for each child. Of course, that's the worst reason."

But I had lost interest in the subject.

"Mom," I said, "let's talk about the triplets."

"Not again," Dad said.

"Please, Mom, tell me the truth. Are you sorry you had them? If you tell me the truth about how you feel, I'll tell you the truth about how I feel."

"OK," Mom said. "If you want to go through it again, I don't mind. For a couple of months there in the beginning, I really was sorry I had them, and maybe I'll tell you something I haven't admitted before—I did not like Randolph at all. Lots of people think that a mother tends to favor the child who needs her the most—and, obviously, that has to be Randolph—but for quite a while, I couldn't stand him."

"I still can't stand him," said Dad.

"Wait a minute, Dad," I told him. "I'm going to get around to you too, but first let Mom finish. Go ahead, Mom. How do you feel now? You can tell the truth."

"Now, I'm not sorry. In fact, I'm happy. Every day I grow happier. It's becoming easier and easier to cope, especially since Mrs. Cole . . ."

"Why do you always have to bring *her* into it?"

"But it's not only the physical help, although I guess I'd be out of my mind if I didn't have it. It's also that I've learned to be patient and to realize that you can't always win. Some days will just turn out to be dog days whatever you do. You have to teach yourself that if one day is bad, there will be lots of others that should be better. And best of all, there are the babies. I love them all now, even Randolph. I couldn't do without any one of them."

I wanted to ask her which one she liked the best. I always wanted to ask her that, but I thought I knew what she would say, and I was afraid.

"What about you, Dad?" I asked.

He hesitated and looked at Mom.

"Come on, Dad," I told him, "tell the truth this time. Are you sorry you have triplets?"

"Yes," Dad admitted, "I am sorry."

"I knew it, I knew it," I said.

"But . . ."

"Oh, don't add any buts. Grownups always add buts, and that's not fair. Just say yes or no."

"Maybe it's the buts that make the difference between children and grownups," Dad went on. "Because although I am sorry I have triplets, I'm really getting used to them now, two of them in particular, and I guess I'm willing to keep them all, even you know who. *But*—and there it is, Dorrie, if I had my way, I would have introduced them one at a time."

"Now I'll tell you what I think," I told them. "And there are no buts with me. I'm sorry they're here. I was a lot happier before they came. Period!"

99

"Don't you think," Mom asked, "that if you took a little more interest in them, you might enjoy yourself, and enjoy them?"

"I doubt it," I told her. "None of them seems very interesting to me. The only one I don't mind, as a matter of fact, is Raymond, and that's because he doesn't bother me as much as the others."

"Well, that's a start," Dad said. "Maybe by the time Raymond is thirty, you might even grow to like him."

"Why don't you like Deirdre?" Mom asked. "She's always so happy when you come near her, and she never disturbs anybody the way Randolph does."

"I like her the least," I said.

"But why?"

Mom had never asked me that question before, although I'm pretty sure she knew how I felt about Deirdre.

"Because she's taking my place. If I died, you wouldn't even miss me now that you have Deirdre. She's beautiful, and I'm not. She's cheerful, and I'm not, and when she grows up to be my age, she won't have the 'Me-Mes,' not her. She'll be perfect."

Nobody laughed this time. Dad even pulled me over into his lap, rubbed my neck, and said, "Poor, little Bunny. Don't you realize that you have one thing that Deirdre and none of the others has?"

"What's that?"

"An eleven years' head start."

It felt good when he said that, and when he kissed me and rolled me around in his lap. I even promised to come out in the yard with him later that morning and help with the weeding, and he promised that the next weekend, he and I, just the two of us, would go out for a night on the town.

But an hour later he was shouting at me because I dropped a couple of jars of applesauce, and that evening, Mom said she didn't like the way I spoke to Genevieve, and that I just had to stop being a selfish, little brat.

It seemed to me that the house was always full of Genevieve. In the beginning, she would go home at dinnertime, but after a while, Mom would say, "If it's all right with your mother, Genevieve, you can stay and have dinner. We're only having meat loaf but . . ."

"I love meat loaf, and my mother said I could stay."

"When did you ask her?" I said.

"I asked her."

"Well, as long as it's all right with her," said my mother with a look at me.

It didn't take long before Genevieve's brother, Harold, started coming over too. He was only ten, a year and a half younger than me, and still in elementary school. He never said much, and Genevieve used to order him around.

Harold

"Harold, here, take this dirty blanket into the laundry room . . . Harold, bring me a bottle of milk . . . Harold, go get Randolph his yellow stuffed dog."

Sometimes Harold went to the store for Mom, and after a while, he started helping Dad work in the garden, and set up a tool bench in the basement.

Soon he was staying very close to Dad, and Dad was always accidentally stepping on his toes or bumping into him. At first, Dad thought it was funny.

"Wherever I go, there's Harold," Dad said. "If I turn around, Harold's behind me, if I open a door, Harold's in front of me, if I look in a dark corner, out comes Harold . . ."

One day, Dad said, he was sitting upstairs looking over some accident reports when he noticed that Harold was standing there in the doorway watching him.

"What is it, Harold?" Dad asked.

Harold shook his head.

"Do you want to ask me something?"

"No."

"Are you looking for something to do?"

"I dunno."

"You can sharpen these pencils for me, Harold. I'd appreciate that."

Harold sharpened the pencils. Then he brought them over to Dad.

"Thanks, Harold," Dad said, reaching out for them. But Harold held onto them, and said, "Is it all right if I hold them, Mr. O'Brien? I could just stand here and give them to you when you need them."

Dad said no, it wasn't all right, but he pulled another chair up to his desk, and gave Harold a list of addresses to check against another list.

"I guess Randolph must take after you," I told Dad.

"Thanks a lot—but what did I do to deserve the compliment?"

"I mean because of the effect the two of you seem to have on the James family. I mean, you don't see anybody following Mom or me around."

I asked Harold one day, "What are you interested in?"

"I dunno."

"What do you want to be when you grow up?"

He smiled and looked away. You could never get him to

look at you if you were looking at him. He shrugged his shoulders.

"Well?"

"I dunno."

"Sure you do. Come on and tell me."

"You'll laugh."

"No, I won't."

"You'll tell."

"No, honestly, I won't tell anybody."

"Not your father."

"I swear."

"OK, I want to be a principal."

I thought it was very funny since Harold was obviously not the principal type, and I told my father. This time he didn't think it was funny, and the following Friday night he took Harold to a basketball game at U.S.F.

"Well, how was it," I asked the next morning.

My father looked grim. "Harold fell asleep during the game, and he cried all the way home because he thought I'd be disappointed in him. This must be the first time an adult ever took him anywhere. Poor kid—what a life he must lead!"

"Maybe he's just not interested in basketball, and that's why he fell asleep."

"I'm sure that's so, and the fact that his mother doesn't see that he gets to bed at a normal time or that he gets enough to eat. I wouldn't be surprised if he's anemic. As a matter of fact, I think I'll just go over to his house tomorrow and have a word with Mrs. James."

"Now, Charlie," Mom said, "you know better than to interfere with a family that—uh—well, let's say a family that has a different life style."

"Oh, come off it, Maureen. I've had plenty of experience with lousy parents. I know how to handle it. I can be very diplomatic when I have to."

Dad went over to Genevieve's house the next day, but Mrs. James was not in. The following evening on his way home from work, Dad tried again, but nobody was home. Both kids were at our house when he came in.

"Genevieve," he said, "I'd like to meet your mother. When would be a good time?"

"She's going out tonight," Genevieve said quickly. "She won't be home until late."

"She's not home now, Genevieve," Dad said.

"Well, maybe she left already."

"Do you think she'll be home tomorrow night? Would you tell her that I'd like to drop over tomorrow night after dinner. Or if it's more convenient, I could come before dinner. I've tried calling, but I never seem to catch her in."

Genevieve looked sulky. She didn't answer my father.

"Genevieve," my father said in his best principal's voice, "will you tell her?"

Genevieve began talking very fast and very angry. "Why do you have to go and see her, Mr. O'Brien? I didn't do anything wrong. Maybe I broke that one bottle, and I didn't tell anybody but honestly I'm going to buy a new one. You don't have to tell my mother—I'll get the money today, right now, and buy another bottle."

Suddenly Harold was crying, and my father said very gently, "Now, Genevieve, that's not why I want to see your mother. You haven't done anything wrong. You've only done everything right, and we all care for you and want you to be happy."

Then Genevieve was crying too. It was the first time I'd ever seen her cry, and she looked funny. Her shoulders were shaking, and her face was all bunched up in lines going up and down and back and forth. The tears came pouring down her nose, and she tried to open her mouth to say something, but all she could do was gasp like a fish.

As soon as Genevieve started crying, Harold began howling. My parents got busy. Mom grabbed Genevieve, and Dad took Harold. For a while, all you could hear were wet sounds and

A Genevievefish ←

Hee Hee!!!

howls. Finally, Harold began to talk, "She's gone . . . it's more than a week now . . . gone."

"Shut up! Shut up!" Genevieve yelled.

But Harold didn't shut up. His mother was gone. He didn't know where but it had been more than a week now—the longest she'd ever been away. She'd taken the big suitcase this time, and left ten dollars on the kitchen table. But now the money was gone, and they didn't have any more food in the house.

"Shut up!" Genevieve kept saying. "Don't listen to him. She'll be back."

Genevieve and Harold had dinner with us that night. It was a good dinner too—roast beef, baked potatoes, and salad. Harold ate a baked potato and laughed at my father's jokes. Genevieve didn't eat anything. She kept crying, and finally Mom said why didn't she go and play some records.

They slept over at our house that night—Harold in Randolph's room, and Genevieve in mine. Mom put air mattresses on the floor for them. I could hear Genevieve crying after the lights were out, and it was easier feeling sorry for her if I didn't have to see her face.

"Genevieve," I said, "don't cry. It'll be all right."

No answer. Just wet sounds.

"Listen, Genevieve," I said, and then didn't know what to say. What *can* you say when somebody's mother just walks out.

"Everybody thinks she's a lousy mother," Genevieve said, "but she's not."

"Oh, no, Genevieve," I lied, "nobody thinks that."

"Yes they do, but they don't know her."

"That's right, Genevieve," I said. "I don't know her. I never even met her. Just once I saw her looking out of the window."

"She's a great mother," Genevieve was crying very hard now. "She loves me and she loves Harold just as much as your mother loves you."

"Sure she does," I said, but Genevieve was crying so hard that I got out of my bed, climbed onto her air mattress, and put an arm around her shoulders. After a while, she fell asleep but I couldn't, so I got up and wandered downstairs.

It was very quiet in the house—wonderfully quiet. The babies were all asleep, and so was everybody else. I was the only one awake. I poured myself some milk and hunted around for cookies. There were some Oreo crumbs in the cookie jar, and, naturally, a box of graham crackers. One thing we never seemed to run out of was graham crackers. As I drank my milk and ate my crackers, I decided that Genevieve had one lousy mother. I wasn't going to say so to her, but I also knew that her mother did not love her as much as my mother loved me.

"It doesn't have to be *that* long," Mrs. Lyons said when I stopped by her desk after class.

I told her, "Jeff Parsons says his is two hundred pages already, and he's going to keep right on until it's longer than *War and Peace*."

"When Jeff Parsons learns to write like Tolstoy," said Mrs. Lyons, "then he can write hundreds and hundreds of pages. But until then I think he should have a little consideration for his English teacher."

I think Mrs. Lyons is sorry now that she gave us a choice. Every kid in the class except for Lorna Ellis, Jack Rose, and Kyoko Matsumoto is writing a book.

The books were due at the end of this week, but I was asking for an extension. "Maybe just another week, at the very most two," I told her, "because I'm still not sure how it's going to end."

"Everybody's asking for an extension," complained Mrs. Lyons. "If I had known for a moment how much writing ability there was in this class I never would have given in to Jeff Parsons."

"Endings are hard," I said. "Everything else was easy, I just wrote it the way it happened. But when you end things, you make them stop, and nothing stops in real life except when you die."

"What's your book about?" Mrs. Lyons asked.

"About me," I told her. "It's a tragedy."

"Another tragedy?" said Mrs. Lyons. "I was hoping at least some of the books would be funny. I cry very easily, and from what I've heard, you're all writing sad stories."

"Parts of my book are funny," I told her. "At least, it may seem funny to you since it's not happening to you. But the real reason I need time to finish the book is that we have house guests—two of them. We've had them for the past week and a half, and I have trouble finding a quiet place to work."

"You don't want to be rude to your guests," Mrs. Lyons said, "so why don't you just hand in what you've written and I won't mind at all that it's not finished. You know, some of the greatest books that have ever been written are unfinished, *Brothers Karamazov*, for example."

But finally she said I could have another two weeks, if I promised not to write more than two hundred pages.

Chapter Ten

It's not going to be easy to finish.

There are no quiet places in my house now at all. I wish Mrs. James would come back, although everybody, except Genevieve, says she won't. Genevieve shares my room and sits at my desk sometimes when I want to do my homework or write my book. Her clothes are hanging in my closet along with my clothes. Yesterday, Mrs. Cole brought over four pairs of boys' pants, two sweaters and three shirts for Harold which she says her boys outgrew. She also brought over a new pink sweater, a new pair of white girl's jeans and a new pair of blue ones. Naturally, she couldn't say her boys outgrew them, and Genevieve didn't ask. But they are hanging in the closet now, along with a new embroidered work shirt my mother bought her, and a new bathrobe. Nobody bought anything new for me.

Genevieve has become very clean. She takes a shower every day, and tells me that I should put my shoes away neatly in the shoebag instead of throwing them under the bed. Mrs. Cole took her for a haircut the other day, and now her hair is real short and curls around her face. I guess she looks OK. I wish her mother would come home. She still cries at night, and then I have to go over to her bed and comfort her. Sometimes she tells me things about her mother—how once she took them down to the boardwalk at Santa Cruz, and another time they all had dinner at a Chinese restaurant. There didn't seem to be much in between, but Genevieve keeps saying over and over again what a great mother she is.

She thinks her mother is looking for a job and will send for them as soon as she finds one.

Harold is beginning to look at me when I ask him questions. I think he's dumb, but Dad says it's because he's anemic and probably suffering from malnutrition. Dr. Holmes told Mom to fatten him up, and she's trying to do that. She wants him to drink lots of milk and eat all the meat he can manage, especially liver. She doesn't like him to drink sodas and eat potato chips, which he loves.

The other day Mom said, "Tonight, we're going out to dinner."

"Who's going out to dinner?" I asked.

"You, Dad and I."

"Just the three of us?"

"That's right."

"How come?" I wanted to know. "It's the middle of the week, and nobody's birthday. And what about Genevieve and Harold? And who's going to look after the babies?"

"Mrs. Cole is coming to baby sit at six-thirty, and both Genevieve and Harold know we're going out."

"Can I wear my long dress?"

"Why not?" Mom smiled. "Maybe I'll dress up too. It'll be fun for a change."

Harold was sitting on the steps playing with a set of plastic cups that belonged to Deirdre. He looked at me as I came down the stairs in my long dress and blue shawl.

"You look nice," he said.

"Thanks, Harold."

"I went to a restaurant once," he said. "I didn't like it. The food was yukky, and I knocked my glass of water over, and Mom yelled. I'm glad I'm not going to a restaurant."

Genevieve was sitting on the living-room rug with Randolph. She had him down on his back, and kept lowering her head into his belly, and making loud "Moo" noises. Randolph was laughing and waving his arms around.

Genevieve looked up as I came into the room, and said,

110

"Mrs. Cole says I can give Randolph a bath tonight. She's going to watch me, but I can do it all by myself."

I was about to say, "Big deal!" but I remembered that tonight I was going out *all by myself* with Mom and Dad, so I smiled at Genevieve and said, "That's great!"

Mom looked pretty. She was wearing her blue Mexican dress with the bright red, green, and yellow embroidered flowers down the front. She wore long silver earrings, and her red hair bounced all around her face. I could smell her

perfume—lately she hardly ever wears perfume any more. I wanted to put my head up against her chest (she always pours a little bit inside the front of her dress), the way I used to, but Genevieve was sitting there watching us so I didn't.

The three of us sat in the front seat of the car with no babies between us. I hadn't felt this good in a long, long time. I told them about the problems I was having ending the book. They knew I was writing it for English, but so far I hadn't shown them any parts or gone into any of the details.

Soon we were seated in a new Chinese restaurant that Dad said he wanted to try. There were good, warm smells all around us. Best of all, we were together, just the three of us, talking about the day that had passed. We had Kuo Teh and sizzling rice soup. After that we had ginger beef, chicken and walnuts and Moo Shu Pork.

"Am I one of the characters in that book of yours?" Dad wanted to know.

"Oh, yes," I told him.

"Am I one of the good guys or one of the bad guys?"

"Sort of half and half," I told him.

"That's encouraging," he said, "and is Mom in it?"

"Uh, huh."

"And the three junior members of the household?"

"The whole story revolves around them," I said. "Not that any one of them is important but if it hadn't been for all of them there wouldn't have been a story."

"And are Genevieve and Harold in it?"

"Oh yes, and that's part of the reason I don't know how to end it. If their mother came back, it would help, but I still would have to work out what's going to happen to the main character." I was helping myself to seconds on the ginger beef. "We ought to do this more often," I told them. "Maybe if we did, my book wouldn't have to be such a tragedy."

"Oh, I don't think it has to be a tragedy at all," Dad said. "In the right hands it could end up a happy family story. A lot depends on the author's point of view."

I took a little more of the chicken and walnuts, and noticed that Mom and Dad had stopped eating. "Don't you want any more?" I asked. "It's so good."

"I'll have some more," Dad said, helping himself, "and I want to ask you something. Actually, your mother and I both want to ask you something, which is one of the reasons why we decided to come out for dinner." He offered Mom the

112

dish, but she shook her head and said, "Dorrie, we have to make a decision about Genevieve and Harold."

"They have a crummy mother," I told them, sprinkling some rice into the puddles of gravy that were still left on my plate. "Genevieve keeps saying how great she is, but I think she must be a stinker."

"Yes," said Dad, "I think so too. And it doesn't look as if she'll be back."

"Genevieve thinks she will," I told him, trying to capture a few grains of rice with my chopsticks.

"I really don't think she does," said Mom, "but she is a child with a fierce sense of loyalty, and I hope she'll be able to find a home, and parents who will deserve that loyalty."

They were looking at me, and I guess I would have to be pretty stupid not to have caught the drift of their conversation.

"What do you want me to say?" I asked.

"It's going to be your decision this time," Dad said. "We both feel you've had a great change in your life because of the triplets, and we know from little things you've let drop, and big things too, that you're angry because you weren't in on the planning."

"And I wasn't," I told them.

"So this time around," said Mom, "we're not going to do anything without your agreement."

I stayed quiet.

"Of course," said Mom, "you ought to think how much happiness you could bring into the lives of two children who haven't had very much."

"But other people," I told them, "could make Genevieve and Harold very happy too. Mrs. Cole is always saying how she wanted a daughter, and another boy shouldn't make a whole lot of difference. Why doesn't Mrs. Cole take them?"

"Mrs. Cole doesn't have any room at all. Her house is smaller than ours, you know. She only has three bedrooms, and I just don't see where she could put them."

"Well, how about Mrs. Wong or Mrs. Esposito."

"Mrs. Wong and Mrs. Esposito are not interested in taking foster children."

"And besides," Dad said, "you have to think about it from Harold and Genevieve's point of view. If they had a choice, I think they would like to stay with us."

"Well, what about you two?" I said. "Do you want to take them?"

"Yes," Mom said, "I do."

"Sure," I told her, "it's because Genevieve is always willing to take Randolph off your back."

"Is that what you think of me?" Mom said. She was very hurt, and her eyelids began blinking fast, the way they always did when she was upset.

"No, no, Mom," I said, reaching over and grabbing her hand. "No, I don't mean that. I know that's not why. I'm sorry."

Dad said slowly, "If I had a real choice maybe I'd say no. The last thing I need in my house is another couple of kids. But they were a part of our family almost before we knew they were—so we don't really have a choice. I mean I don't feel I have a choice, Dorrie. You're the one who's making the decision."

"They're dumb kids," I said, "and Genevieve is all over the place."

Nobody said anything.

"Nothing is my own any more. Her clothes are in my closet, she uses my desk, there's no place I can go that just belongs to me."

"Whatever you decide," Mom said, "we'll understand. You won't have to feel guilty."

"Now why are you saying that?" I said. "You know I'm going to feel guilty if I don't say yes, don't you?"

"Yes," Mom said, "I'm sure you would, but it's up to you, and Dad and I aren't going to put any pressure on you."

"Sure you're going to put pressure on me. That's why you took me out to dinner tonight. And you know, don't you, that if we take Genevieve and Harold, we'll never be able to get out like this—just the three of us. Never! We'll have to put up with Harold knocking his water over us, and Genevieve talking about what a great mother she has."

Dad said, "I'm sure we'd be able to work something out. We're all going to need time off from one another anyway, even without Genevieve and Harold. Maybe there isn't that much difference between a family of six and a family of eight. I'm sure there won't be nearly as much difference as between a family of three and a family of six."

The waiter brought us some fortune cookies. Mine said "Your name will be on the lips of thousands," which didn't have anything to do with making a decision.

"I don't think it's fair to do this to me," I told them. "Don't Genevieve or Harold have relatives or friends of the family?"

"No," said Dad, "I've checked everything out. They have no one."

"It's never going to end," I told them. "Anybody that needs a place to stay—all the homeless cats and dogs—what about them?"

"I guess we'd have to stop with Genevieve and Harold," Mom said. "We just don't have any more room—well, maybe we could manage to squeeze in a cat or a dog."

"Very funny," I said, "but I've had just about all I can stand."

"That's right," Mom said sympathetically.

"And I just don't want any more people in the house."

Dad paid the check.

"Enough is enough, and there are plenty of other people who can be nice to them."

Dad and Mom were quiet as we drove back home.

"They can come over and visit us sometimes, and maybe sleep over every once in a while. It's not like they'll never see us again. And who knows, maybe their mother *will* come back."

Dad parked the car, but before we got out I yelled at them,

"You knew very well, didn't you, what I was going to decide. You really stacked the cards against me, didn't you? I never really had a choice, and you know it. It's just not fair, it's not fair."

Mom kissed me. "There was only one possible decision, Dorrie, but we hoped you would realize it without our telling you."

Dad said, patting my head, "Maybe now, you'll be able to put a happy ending on that book of yours."

Chapter Eleven

I always knew that there was somebody buried out in the yard. Genevieve said that there wasn't. She said she was only trying to scare me that day I first met her, and that it was all a big joke. Mom said I was letting my imagination run away with me, and Dad said if I did more weeding and less talking the yard might actually turn into a garden. Nobody would listen to me, not even Harold.

But I knew.

There was an arrow on the old retaining wall that Dad planned to remove and replace with a redwood fence. The arrow was an old one. It had been scratched into the wall and

it pointed downward. Next to it was a line of numbers starting at one, and continuing at least up until ten. Part of the wall had collapsed, and possibly there had been more numbers scratched into the missing part.

I tried pointing out the arrow and the numbers to different members of my family and foster family, but nobody would listen. This is usually the case with people who make unusual discoveries.

One night when the moon was full, I woke up and knew that the time had come. I dressed myself very carefully because Genevieve was tossing restlessly in her new bed with the matching quilt and pillow set. It isn't nearly as pretty as my quilt, and of course it's not an authentic patchwork either, but she seems satisfied with it. Especially since the pillowcase has the same design. My whole room has been rearranged. I guess I should say *our* whole room has been rearranged. Genevieve doesn't sleep on an air mattress any more. She has a bed with a headboard that she picked out herself, and a new desk which is larger than mine, but I don't think is anywhere as pretty. Genevieve's desk is always neat, and her bed is always made. She keeps an old stuffed bear on her bed—she sleeps with it. Isn't that ridiculous? A girl who's thirteen and a half still sleeping with a stuffed animal! She always hangs her clothes up and puts her shoes away in the shoebag. So her half of the room is a lot neater than mine and a lot less interesting.

I got into an old pair of jeans, an old sweat shirt, and carrying my sneakers, I walked barefoot out of the room. Carefully, I tiptoed downstairs and peeped into the living room. Sure enough, Harold was stretched out on one of the sofas. Sometimes Harold can't sleep at night, and he tends to wander. Sometimes he'll fall asleep on one of the sofas, sometimes on the rug, and sometimes sitting in a kitchen chair with his head down on the table. It's really amazing that he doesn't wake Randolph since they share a room. Randolph, by the way, doesn't wake up much at night any more. He still screams a lot during the day except when Genevieve is around. She plays with him, carries him around, and keeps stuffing food into his mouth when he won't stop yelling. He's going to be spoiled rotten because of all the attention Genevieve gives him. If she has to be making a fuss over somebody why doesn't she concentrate on Harold? He all the details. I know you don't want to be bothered."

Mom came running down the stairs. She was holding Deirdre, and she looked at me and the two policemen, and cried, "Oh—is everything all right? Dorrie, darling, what's happened?"

"Don't worry, Mom," I told her cheerfully. "You're busy with Deirdre, but it's OK. I'll handle everything."

Then Genevieve came down the stairs. I told her, "There is a body in the yard."

"I don't believe it," Genevieve said.

I shrugged my shoulders, smiled at the policemen, and said, "This way, gentlemen."

Harold came running in from the living room. He didn't say anything, but he followed after us as we went down into the cellar and out into the yard. The light was stronger now, and the skeleton hand could be seen clearly. Its fingers were curling inward. One of the policemen took out his book and began to write. The other one asked if he could use the phone, and I led him back to the kitchen and offered to make some coffee for him and his partner.

Later the chief inspector came out and brought a digging crew with him. It wasn't long before they dug up the rest of the body that was attached to the hand. The inspector was not in uniform. He wore a suit and a raincoat. He stood outside in the yard, supervising the digging operation, and he had a worried look on his face.

I approached him, and said, "Inspector."

"Yes," he replied, and looked at me. There was kindness and intelligence in his face, and a deep look of sorrow in his eyes.

"I would like to show you some numbers, Inspector, that might be very valuable clues."

"Numbers?" he repeated.

"Yes, Inspector, numbers. Please step this way."

I led him to the retaining wall and pointed out the line of numbers, each one about a foot away from the other. He was

really needs it. He's so quiet, most of the time nobody notices him. Genevieve is always bossing him around. Harold, do this and Harold, do that. You don't see her playing with him or stuffing any food into *his* mouth. And he can certainly use it. He's been here a month, and in spite of all the milk and liver and mashed potatoes Mom has been feeding him he still looks like a broomstick.

Harold lay curled up on the sofa, one of his slippers still on. He was folded up around himself because it was pretty cold in the house. There weren't any blankets downstairs, so I took Mom's long coat out of the closet and spread it over him.

I put on the light that led down to the cellar and walked slowly down the stairs. They were old and creaky, and I was afraid that one of my parents would wake up. That would be the end of my plan. Down in the cellar, I looked through Dad's shovels, and selected a large one.

Now came the spooky part. I opened the door that led from the cellar into the yard. The cold night air blew against my face, and I thought about my warm, safe bed. It would be so easy to turn around and go back upstairs, but I knew that if I did, nobody would ever find out the truth.

It was absolutely silent in the yard. The moonlight spread a pale, eerie light over everything. Why, I asked myself, do you have to be the one? You're only eleven and a half, and not very strong, and not generally considered very brave. Go back, I told myself, go back to your warm, safe bed and leave the truth to others.

But I knew it was up to me, so I held the shovel tight in my hands, took a deep breath, and stepped out into the yard. The arrow and numbers seemed to be even sharper in the moonlight. I began to dig right in the spot where the arrow pointed. The earth was hard, and the shovel seemed very heavy.

Many times during that dig, I was on the point of stopping. Sometimes I heard sounds out in that quiet, lonely yard that sounded like no sounds I'd ever heard in my whole life. Sometimes, my hands felt raw and numb. There were blisters on both palms, large, red, tender blisters. And how slowly the hole grew in the earth! The shovel was so heavy, thinking about it now, it's hard for me to really believe that I had the strength, courage, and will to go on.

But I did! All that night I dug, as the moon moved across the sky and finally disappeared. For a while I dug in the dark, my hands like torn and bleeding sores. Slowly, the shovel dug deeper and deeper into the earth. I was down two feet, maybe three. The darkness began to pale. Dawn was about to break. If I was mistaken, how could I explain that deep hole to Dad? What would he say? What would he do?

A bird began to sing. There were only a few very bright stars in the sky, and the faint light of morning spread over the yard. Every part of my body was aching now. Just one more spadeful of earth and no more . . . just another . . . I was about ready to collapse . . . just one more, and I would give up.

There was something in the earth that my shovel hit, something that made a sharp sound against the metal. I had to bend over to see it for the morning light was just beginning to fill up the hole I had dug. Now I could see it clearly, stretching up toward me—a hand, a skeleton hand that seemed to come straight up out of the earth.

I dug no further. It was time to turn the job over to other hands than mine, stronger and older hands. I walked up the cellar steps and into the kitchen. I picked up the phone and dialed the number I had already memorized for the time when I knew I would need it.

"Hello? Police?" I said. "This is Dorrie O'Brien. I have just discovered a body in my yard, and I think you had better come over right away."

In five minutes they were knocking at the door—two big policemen. I let them in. "Right this way, officers," I told them.

Dad came down the stairs just at that moment, his face still puffy from sleep. He looked at the two policemen and he looked at me, and suddenly he was completely awake.

"What is it? What's happened?" he cried. He looked frightened, and I said kindly, "It's all right, Dad, there is a body in the yard, but I'll take the officers out and give them

puzzled. He looked at the numbers, and then he looked at me. "You said clues," he said. "What do you think they mean?"

I told him. "Inspector, I'm afraid there may be more than one body in this yard."

Of course, I was right. By the end of the day, eleven other bodies had been dug up—one under each of the numbers in the retaining wall.

"Inspector," I said.

"Yes."

"I don't believe you're finished yet."

"What do you mean?"

"Look over at that retaining wall, Inspector. You see how the wall has crumbled away over there at the end of the yard?"

"Ah, yes," said the inspector, "you think there might be something buried there?"

"Yes, I do."

"Another body?"

"Perhaps. Perhaps not. Have your men measure a foot from the last body, and see what you find."

He looked at me, and the look of sorrow was strong in his eyes.

"You have a fine mind," he said. "There are very few people in our department who have brilliant minds, and we need more. I have no children—my wife and I have wanted a child but to no avail." (The look in his eyes was heartbreaking) "But if I had a child like you, I believe I could make a master detective of her. How I wish I did!"

"Thank you, Inspector," I said. "Perhaps some arrangement could be made. But for now, I think your crew should get busy."

And they did. And of course there *was* something buried right in the corner of the yard—not a body—but a large metal box filled with jewels and rare and precious stones that gleamed and glittered when the box was opened.

In a few days, the mystery had been solved. The eleven
men who were buried in the yard were once part of the
dreaded gang of jewel thieves known as the "Dead Hands."
They had robbed rare and precious jewels from stores,
palaces, mansions, and museums. Their leader, Winston
Burton, had lived alone in our house under an assumed name.
This was all back in the twenties. Eventually, he killed all the
members of his gang—one by one—and buried them out in
the yard. He wanted to have the jewels all to himself. They

were also buried out in the yard where he had placed them for safekeeping until he had murdered all the other members of the gang. But Fate caught up with him. On the day after he had killed and buried the last member of his gang, he died suddenly of a heart attack.

The jewels were worth millions of dollars, and the rewards came to one hundred thousand dollars. I received the money on the same day the mayor awarded me a special medal for bravery and unusual service.

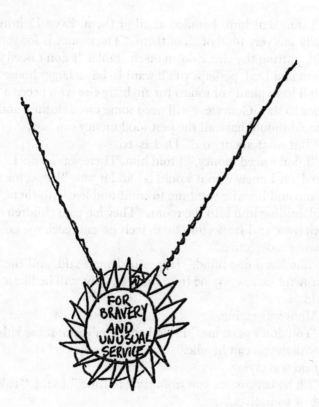

When I returned from the ceremony, they were all waiting for me in the living room.

"I am so proud of you, Dorrie," Mom said. "I only wish I had listened to you earlier."

"Me too," said Dad. "And I apologize for all the times I was too busy to hear what you had to say."

"You were right," Genevieve said, "and I'll try to stop pointing out to you how messy your side of the room looks."

"What will you do with the money?" Harold wanted to know.

I smiled at him. I smiled at all of them. Even Deirdre. I really was very fond of all of them. "The money is for you," I said, putting the check down on the table. "I don't need it. Mom and Dad, perhaps you'll want to buy a larger house so you'll have plenty of rooms for anybody else who needs a place to stay. Genevieve will need some more clothes, and Harold should have all the best food money can buy."

"But what about you?" Dad asked.

"I don't need money," I told him. There was a knock on the door. I knew who it would be, and it was. "Inspector Doran and his wife want me to come and live with them," I said, leading him into the room. "They have no children of their own, and Inspector Doran feels he can teach me how to become a detective."

"She has a fine mind," Inspector Doran said, and the sorrowful look was gone from his eyes. "She will be like a child to us."

Mom was crying.

"You don't need me," I told her. "You've got more kids now than you can handle."

Dad was crying.

"I'll be back to see you from time to time," I said. "Take care of yourselves."

Genevieve and Harold were crying.

"I hope you enjoy my room, Genevieve. Now it's all yours."

Raymond, Randolph, and Deirdre were crying too as I slipped my hand into Inspector Doran's hand and quietly closed the door behind me.

THE END

AFTER

Mrs. Lyons didn't like my ending. She handed all the books back the day before yesterday, and I was the only one in the whole class who got an A. Mrs. Lyons wrote on the first page, "It would have been an A+ if you hadn't written such a contrived ending."

She read parts of my book to the class, and some of the kids told me they really liked it. Not Jeff Parsons because he got a B— on his book even though it was 273 pages long and all about two doctors in the Vietnam war. Mrs. Lyons thought it sounded a lot like M*A*S*H, which is about two doctors in the Korean war. Most of the kids got B's and C's but a few, like Steve Bosco and Cindy Zimmerman, got F's. They will have to read King Arthur after all, and write a book report on it if they want to raise their marks.

I went up to talk to Mrs. Lyons after class. "I liked the ending," I told her. "I think it's the best part of the book."

"Maybe it could be the best part of another book," she said, "but it really doesn't fit with the rest of this book."

"Why not?"

"Well, most of the story is autobiographical and based on real happenings, am I right?"

"Yes."

"The last chapter is made up, and doesn't really relate to the rest of the book. Most of your story deals with a family that has problems but your last chapter suddenly turns it into a whodunit and a fantasy. An ending has to be part of the whole, but it also has to pull everything together, tie up all the loose ends, and bring some sense into what's gone before."

"Suppose it isn't possible to bring any sense into what's gone before? Suppose all you're left with is loose ends?"

"That may happen in real life, but if you're writing a story, you have to make sense out of what's gone before, and find one loose end at least to tie up all the others."

"That's what I tried to do," I told her. "And the only way I could pull everything together was to make up an ending. Because in my real life, there isn't going to be an ending that will make any kind of sense."

Then Mrs. Lyons said never mind, and that it really was very good for a first attempt, and that she planned to show it to Mr. Chin, the principal. She said maybe by the time I finished my second book, I'd find it easier to write a proper ending.

I don't want to wait until I write a second book to have a proper ending. So I asked Dad to read it and tell me what he thought. He was working on a speech he was planning to give to a bunch of other principals later in the week, and he said he'd read it over the weekend.

"Can't you read it sooner?"

"I'd really like to, Bunny, but this is an important talk, and I'm going to need the next few evenings to get it done."

"Oh . . . sure, Dad . . . that's . . . all right." I guess I said it in my new sad, weak voice, which lately seems to work better on him than yells or complaints.

Later he started reading my book.

I kept tiptoeing into his room and looking over his shoulder while he read. Sometimes I just hung around outside the door, and if I heard him laugh, I'd rush in to see what part he was reading. He laughed a lot, particularly during the last chapter. After a while I just stayed behind him and read along over his shoulder until he turned the final page.

"Well?" I asked him. "What do you think?"

130

"It's hilarious," he said, "the funniest thing I've ever read."

"Mrs. Lyons didn't like the last chapter," I told him. "What do you think?"

"I think the last chapter is wonderful. It's a real happy ending. The family is one hundred thousand dollars richer, and manages to get rid of the worst kid of the bunch—it's my favorite part of the book."

"Dad!"

"And what's with this mean father who never has any time for his poor, neglected daughter?" he asked, putting his arm around me. "What a villain the man is! If I had a father like that I'd run away from home. The author, I notice, doesn't have one nice thing to say about him."

"There isn't much nice to say about him," I said, dropping into his lap, and snuggling against his shoulder. "But she did say that he was better-looking than Robert Redford, and that he used to make delicious Caesar salads."

"She didn't say what he thought of his daughter," said my father, squeezing me so hard I had to gasp.

"She knows what he thinks of her," I said in a squashed voice, "and it makes her very unhappy."

"That's good," said my father, "so I won't have to waste my time telling her, because I'm a very busy man, and if a certain eminent author doesn't get off my lap and get lost, she's going to get pinched in a very sensitive spot."

My father was really no help at all.

The next day Mom read it, and she wasn't much help either. For one thing she didn't think it was funny at all, the way Dad did, and she also didn't care for the way the mother in the story was portrayed.

"You make her sound as if she doesn't care at all that her oldest child is unhappy."

"Well, she didn't seem to notice."

"That is really ridiculous," said my mother angrily. "Of course she noticed, and worried, and did everything she could to show her daughter how much she loved her. You didn't put any of that in—how the mother talked to her daughter over and over again, how she reassured her, how she always tried to find time at night to be alone with her even though there were times she was so tired she could hardly keep her eyes open."

"But, Mom, what did you think of the ending?"

"I thought it was stupid," my mother said. "You don't think any decent mother is going to let her daughter go off into the sunset with a strange police inspector and his wife."

"Mrs. Lyons says it doesn't go along with the rest of the book."

"Of course, it doesn't," said my mother. "I think a good ending would have the main character develop into a more considerate person."

"I don't think I care for that kind of an ending."

"Well, then, maybe you could have the main character, because it really is *her* problem, develop an interest in other members of the family. Of course, you haven't seen fit to develop any of the other characters in your book, and the mother in particular seems bland and kind of sappy."

"Who could the main character develop an interest in?"

"There are plenty of people in her family. I would think she has quite a choice—maybe her mother, her father, or better yet, her sisters and brothers."

"Oh, them!"

Mom was getting kind of steamed up so I went off and began thinking that maybe I should try her suggestion and see if I couldn't develop some interest in the triplets. I decided to start with Deirdre. She was napping, and I tiptoed into her room and looked down at her in the crib. Her thumb was in her mouth, and her face was glowing and rosy. I decided I didn't want to develop any interest in her, or maybe I was already too interested in her. At any rate, for the time being, the best thing was not to think about Deirdre at all.

Randolph was being entertained by Genevieve outside the house. She had him propped up in a stroller and was zooming up and down the street with him. I decided I didn't want to think about him either.

Which left Raymond, who was just finishing a jar of strained carrots that Mrs. Cole was feeding him. Raymond, I decided, was going to be the neglected one of the triplets. Deirdre was the beauty and Randolph was the loudmouth. People noticed them, but Raymond was kind of lost in the shuffle. He was chubby too, and would probably end up with a weight problem, and I knew—from personal experience— how miserable that could be.

"Here, Mrs. Cole," I said, "why don't I finish feeding him?"

"Oh, that's fine, Dorrie, he's really hungry today."

Raymond wriggled in his chair and laughed up at me.

"Here we go," I told him, and put the spoon into his mouth. There were pieces of carrots all over the inside of his mouth and all the way down his throat. He put up his hand and wiped some carrot pieces across his eye. What a mess! I decided that maybe one day in the future I'd get interested in Raymond—one day when he had passed the mashed-carrots stage. I finished feeding him, wiped his face and hands, and came upstairs to finish this.

Maybe there is no finish, and maybe, in spite of what Mrs. Lyons says, I will just have to end without an ending. I've been sitting here thinking for a long time now, and Mom is calling me to come down for dinner. "In a minute," I tell her. "In a minute." But now Dad is calling, and he's saying, "Not in a minute. Right now!" so I'd better go. Maybe I'll wait until after dinner before I give up on finding an ending.

AFTER DINNER

Now I am going to finish. Everybody is still downstairs. Dad and Genevieve are doing the dishes, Mom is busy with one baby or another, and Harold is watching TV. There is nothing really further to add. I told them at dinner that my book was going to be an unfinished one, and Dad said, good, that I should give up writing, become a banker, and make a lot of money.

Mom said Harold should eat his grapefruit, and that even though she hadn't liked the character of the mother in the book, she admired many things about it. She wanted me to understand that she was very proud of me for writing it, and that she thought it was an amazing piece of work for a person who wasn't even twelve. And that Harold should put some butter on his bread.

Dad asked her what she thought of the character of the father in the story.

"What father?" Mom asked. "Was there a father in the story? I didn't notice the minor characters, and, Harold, try some of that creamed spinach. It's good for you."

"No," Harold said.

"Just take a taste," Mom urged.

"No," yelled Harold. "I hate it, and stop nagging me. Stop it!"

He slammed his plate back on the table, right into mine, and my baked potato came leaping up into my lap.

All of us looked at Harold in astonishment. He was glaring at my mother, his face really red with anger. As I guess I didn't mention before, Harold was so quiet you hardly ever knew he was around. And he was never fresh, never answered back, and never misbehaved.

This was the first time.

Finally Dad reached over, grabbed Harold's shoulder and said, "Now just cut that out, young man."

"You leave me alone too," Harold shouted.

Genevieve said, "You better tell Maureen you're sorry, Harold. You've got some nerve!"

"You shut up," Harold yelled at her, and he kicked the table with both feet.

"Why don't you all stop picking on him," I yelled. "All of

you. All you ever do is tell him what to do—eat this, eat that, go here, go there—leave him alone!"

"Leave me alone!" Harold yelled at me.

"Why are you yelling, 'Leave me alone!' to me?" I said. "I'm on your side, you dope."

"All right, Harold," Mom said, "you don't have to eat the spinach if you don't want to. I didn't know you felt so strongly about it. You never said anything."

"I hate it!" said Harold.

"Well, you don't have to eat anything you hate."

"And I hate string beans, and rice, and cottage cheese. I hate rye bread, liver, mayonnaise, and grape jam, and I hate . . ."

There seemed to be lots of things Harold hated, and for the first time he let everybody know it. I think it's a good thing Harold got sore and lost his temper. Maybe he's been afraid to get angry before this but now he knows he's got a real family, and in a real family everybody's allowed to get mad from time to time.

Yesterday, the license arrived saying that Mom and Dad could be foster parents. It's only good for a year, and then it has to be renewed.

"I'll gladly go through another physical," Dad said, "but I'm not going to be fingerprinted again—and I'll tell them so too."

"You already have, Charlie," Mom said, "loud and clear."

"I just can't understand," Dad said, really warming up, "why people who want foster children have to be treated like common criminals."

Harold was listening. He looked at Dad, and then he said, "What would happen if they say you have to be fingerprinted again?"

"I'm going to blow my top," said Dad.

"But what if they still say you have to."

"They better not."

"But suppose they do. What would happen if they do, and

you won't let them? What would happen then?"

"You're really full of whats today, Harold," Mom said, laughing. But you could see that Harold was looking nervous. Dad said, "If they said I had to, I'd let them know what I think. And you know, Harold, I've already written a letter to the agency asking them to change their policy, but if they kept on insisting, I guess I'd just have to let them fingerprint me. Because if I didn't, I wouldn't be able to be a foster parent, and if I wasn't able to be a foster parent, I wouldn't be able to have you and Genevieve as foster children."

Harold was still watching Dad.

"Does that answer your question, Harold?"

Harold didn't say anything, but he kept watching Dad. Dad laughed and looked nervous too. He's not used to boys yet. So he said to Harold, "Your shirt's sticking out again. Come here, I'll fix it for you." He pulled Harold over to him, poked at his shirt, patted him on his shoulder, and Harold leaned against him—and I guess that answered his question.

Maybe Harold isn't as dumb as I thought. Maybe he's the one I ought to take an interest in. A neglected boy who seems dumb on the outside, but who really has great talents buried down deep just waiting to be dug up. Who knows? I could be the one who encourages him and guides him and helps develop his talents. Whatever they are. And, besides, Harold is past the strained-carrot stage.

Maybe I'll go downstairs now and teach Harold how to play Monopoly. I guess Genevieve can play too if she wants. Maybe Harold won't want to play Monopoly with me. Maybe he won't want me to help develop his talents. Maybe he just wants me to leave him alone.

I guess I could do that too.

The only thing I can't do, is finish this story.

Last Page

MARILYN SACHS, a native New Yorker, received her Bachelor of Arts degree from Hunter College and a Master's degree in Library Science from Columbia University. As a specialist in children's literature, she was with the Brooklyn Public Library for more than ten years and with the San Francisco Public Library for five years. She now devotes full time to writing and is recognized as an outstanding children's book author. *The Bears' House* was a 1971 nominee in children's books for the National Book Award. *Veronica Ganz* and *A Pocket Full of Seeds* were selected by the American Library Association as Notable Children's Books of the Year.

Mrs. Sachs lives in San Francisco with her husband, Morris, her son, Paul, and her daughter, Anne.

ANNE SACHS is a college freshman who is interested in people, books, politics, art, dancing, baseball, hiking, biking, serious conversations, funny conversations, food, diets, and music. This is the first book she has illustrated and she says, "It may be the last."